D0920894

I walked slowly toward them

L A N D

O F   T E R R O R

by

EDGAR RICE BURROUGHS

Illustrated by ROY G. KRENKEL

Introduction to the Bison Books Edition by
Anne Harris

UNIVERSITY OF NEBRASKA PRESS
LINCOLN AND LONDON

Copyright © 1944 by Edgar Rice Burroughs, Inc.
Introduction © 2007 by Edgar Rice Burroughs, Inc.
All rights reserved
Manufactured in the United States of America

First Nebraska paperback printing: 2007

Library of Congress Cataloging-in-Publication Data
Burroughs, Edgar Rice, 1875–1950
Land of terror / Edgar Rice Burroughs; illustrated by Roy G.
Krenkel; introduction to the Bison Books edition by Anne Harris.
p.   cm.
ISBN-13: 978-0-8032-6265-2 (pbk.: alk. paper)
ISBN-10: 0-8032-6265-5 (pbk.: alk. paper)
1. Earth—Core—Fiction.   I. Krenkel, Roy G., 1918–   II. Title.
PS3503.U687L34   2007
813'.52—dc22   2006102649

This Bison Books edition follows the original in beginning chapter
1 on arabic page 9; no material has been omitted.

INTRODUCTION

Anne Harris

It isn't easy being a feminist and a Burroughs fan. *Land of Terror*, the sixth book in the Pellucidar series, is particularly challenging, not only to feminist views but also to many other contemporary perspectives. That's not to say that it isn't worth reading, however. It is, for both its considerable entertainment value and for what it has to say about who we were and who we are now.

Unlike many devotees of his work, I did not discover Edgar Rice Burroughs as a wide-eyed innocent. I was thirty years old, an adult with well-formed late twentieth-century liberal sensibilities and a reasonable familiarity with modern science fiction, when I picked up *A Princess of Mars* and *The Gods of Mars*, the first two volumes of the Barsoom series. I realized his science was out to lunch and his values were paternalistic, but it didn't matter. I was instantly swept away in the nonstop action, the vivid detail, and, best of all, the unfettered imagination of Burroughs's writing.

The culture of the warlike, communist, four-armed Tharks—anthropologically iffy. John Carter's notion of honor—dicey from a feminist perspective. Blue, humanoid plant creatures that feed on red grass—ecologically suspect. But I didn't care because I was right there in the thick of things with Carter and—Ooh! Look! Purple trees!

In his introduction to an earlier Bison Books release, *Pellucidar*, science fiction author Jack McDevitt credits Burroughs's success to his ability to make the reader feel what the protagonist feels. I think this is very true. I also agree with McDevitt's assertion that this empathy is the reason readers are so willing to forgive Burroughs his shortcomings. We're too busy fighting banths and escaping from giant ants to question the science, the lack thereof, or the philosophical underpinnings of it all.

Pellucidar is a world beneath our world. In the first Pellucidar book, *At the Earth's Core*, David Innes and Abner Perry set out in an invention of Perry's, the Iron Mole, which bores into the earth. Their intention is to prospect for coal, but instead they break through the earth at a depth of five hundred miles and find themselves on the inside of a hollow world—a vast, horizonless landscape with an unmoving sun at its center. It is always noon in Pellucidar.

The physics of this world are impossible. Gravity should cause everything on the inner surface of Pellucidar to fall into the central sun. Furthermore, Burroughs equates the lack of moving celestial bodies with the actual stoppage of time. Because there is no way to record time, he reasons, time does not elapse. Through countless adventures, as years pass on the surface world, Innes and Perry do not age. Which is a good thing because, lacking the homing instinct that all Pellucidarans are born with and with no horizon or stars to guide them, Innes and Perry get lost a lot.

But that is one of the principle joys of the Pellucidar books—the boundless prospect of adventure, unfettered even by common sense. There's something about Burroughs's disregard for, and at times open rebellion against, what is actually possible that I find inspiring. His tales are a frank break from the expected. His intent is to take you for the wildest ride that he can, and if logic is going to interfere with that, then logic can catch a mastodon cab for the surface world. It's Edgar's party down here.

As an author, I have long wished to do what Burroughs does, but alas the pulps are no more. Science fiction has grown up, and we all have to make sense now. Of course, it is desirable and inevitable that a genre mature, becoming self-critical and sophisticated. But still, if I had my own Burroughsian device, such as the Iron Mole or Carter's celestial teleportation, I just might use it to transport myself to the pulp era and write scads of stories full of weird creatures, strange landscapes, and deadly peril.

Pellucidar is populated by dinosaurs, woolly mammoths, and saber-toothed tigers. Neolithic humans are enslaved by intelligent, bipedal reptiles called "Mahars." Until, that is, Perry fashions gunpowder, guns, and a naval fleet, and Innes frees the humans, defeats the Mahars, and becomes emperor of Pellucidar.

Perry's development of gunpowder is one of those passages in *Land of Terror* that brings the contrast between Burroughs's era and ours into sharp relief. Innes tells us: "They used to kill each other with stone hatchets and stone-shod spears before we came, and only a few tribes had even bows and arrows; but we have taught them how to make gunpowder and rifles and cannon, and they are commencing to realize the advantages of civilization" (11).

Innes and Perry often equate gunpowder with civilization.

Nowadays, gunpowder and all that goes with it seem more likely to cause civilization's downfall. One has to wonder if Burroughs didn't hold the same opinion when the novel was published in 1941. Certainly the author's tongue is firmly in his cheek when Innes observes: "When I left Sari on this expedition I am about to tell you of, Perry was trying to perfect poison gas. He claimed that it would do even more to bring civilization to the Old Stone Age" (12).

Perhaps the explanation lies with Burroughs's oft-observed antipathy toward civilization itself. As Innes and his companions make their way back to their home country of Sari at the start of *Land of Terror*, they encounter a landscape devoid of human habitation. Innes describes the experience as the height of adventure, and later in the same section he states, "Man had not yet come to bring discord to this living idyl" (15). Alternatively, McDevitt ascribes a pragmatic motive to Burroughs's attitude toward civilization, noting that Innes, Carter, and Tarzan—all independent men of action—are at their best when engaged in a stark struggle for survival.

But most telling of all is this inside jacket copy for *Tiger Girl*, which was later combined with three other tales and published as *Savage Pellucidar*, the last in the Pellucidar series: "It will take you to strange lands across the nameless strait in the Stone Age world at the Earth's Core, and to adventures upon the terrible seas of Pellucidar. It will take you from the terrors with which you have been for years accustomed—the terrors of a world gone mad with hate—to the cleaner, finer terrors of prehistoric hunting beasts and savage, primeval man."

Needless to say, as the creator of Tarzan, Burroughs strongly shaped the concept of the noble savage, and this ideal is expressed again in *Land of Terror*. Innes extols the achievements of early humans: "If you think the first steam engine was a marvel of ingenuity, how much more ingenuity must it have taken to conceive and make the first stone knife" (27).

But not all of Burroughs's savages are noble; the tribes who capture Innes and his cohorts are most decidedly ignoble. The Jukans, for instance, are mad by the definition of Burroughs's time. They provide a striking glimpse of mid-twentieth-century views on mental and emotional disorders. The scene where Innes is led through the village as a captive is the most chilling in the book, giant insects notwithstanding.

At the outset of *Land of Terror*, Innes is captured by a tribe of large, hulking brutes with big bushy beards and names such as "Rhump." He is not with them long before he discovers that they are women. They take him to their village, where he encounters the males of the tribe—waifish, mewling creatures with names that all end in the letter *a*. It is obvious that Burroughs has simply taken gross caricatures of males and females and switched their designations. The "women" are men, and the "men" are women. But what is his purpose for the switch-up?

The answer becomes clear before long:

> If these women were the result of taking women out of slavery and attempting to raise them to equality with man, then I think that they and the world would be better off if they were returned to slavery. One of the sexes must rule; and man seems temperamentally better fitted for the job than woman. Certainly if full power over man has resulted in debauching

and brutalizing women to such an extent, then we should see
that they remain always subservient to man, whose overlordship is, more often than not, tempered by gentleness and sympathy. (36)

The passage has the virtue of blatancy. Now that such state-
ments are no longer acceptable when voiced in so straight-
forward a manner, they often find their way into art and entertainment in much sneakier ways. One wonders uneasily
sometimes, "Is this sexist? What *is* the author's intent here?"
Burroughs's intent is perfectly plain, and though I can only
deplore it, I find some comfort in the fact that it is right in
front of me where I can point to it and say, "Oh yeah, that's
right; this is why I'm a feminist."

Still, reading this passage for the first time was the cogni-
tive equivalent of walking along a path in the jungle, admiring
the scenery, and suddenly falling through the cleverly cam-
ouflaged opening of a tiger pit onto the cruel stakes of sexism
laid below. But I should have known what jungle I was in to
begin with. After all, Burroughs wrote for a largely male au-
dience in the first half of the twentieth century. Although he
provides us with strong characters such as Dejah Thoris and
Dian the Beautiful—capable women who have the ability to
deal with their aggressors—Burroughs also makes sure that
they are always available to be rescued by the men who love
them.

I had allowed myself to be diverted by Burroughs's entertaining writing and forgot that he was not writing for me. Perhaps one of the most valuable things about this new edition
of *Land of Terror* is that it serves as a reminder of just how

much popular sentiment regarding women's role in society has changed since the book's original publication in 1941.

It's probably best not to take anything in *Land of Terror* too seriously. By the law of gravity, everyone and everything in Pellucidar should plummet into the central sun. Should we take Burroughs's assertions concerning women, the mentally ill, indigenous people, or warfare any more to heart than his notion that centrifugal force can counteract gravity? It is more useful to read these elements in the spirit of historical awareness—notice them, acknowledge them, and then get back to the fun.

And thankfully, Burroughs soon abandons social commentary and gets down to what he excels at: telling a ripping adventure story full of daring escapes, strange creatures, and exotic landscapes. There aren't any purple trees in Pellucidar, but there are floating islands, giant ants, and saber-toothed tigers.

The text includes the wonderful illustrations by Roy G. Krenkel from the Canaveral Press editions of the early sixties. The dynamism of these images is a perfect match to Burroughs's writing. Burroughs's sentences are full of momentum, carrying the reader effortlessly through all of the redoubtable David Innes's adventures. Innes grapples with each new danger with characteristic humor and spirit, making friends with noble savages and woolly mammoths, rescuing Dian the Beautiful, losing her, and finding her again. All in all, it is a fun ride.

Enjoy *Land of Terror* for all of its virtues as well as its vices.

LIST OF ILLUSTRATIONS

≍ I ≍

W H E N Jason Gridley got in touch with me recently by radio and told me it was The Year of Our Lord Nineteen Hundred and Thirty-nine on the outer crust, I could scarcely believe him, for it seems scarcely any time at all since Abner Perry and I bored our way through the Earth's crust to the inner world in the great iron mole that Perry had invented for the purpose of prospecting for minerals just beneath the surface of the Earth. It rather floored me to realize that we have been down here in Pellucidar for thirty-six years.

You see, in a world where there are no stars and

no moon, and a stationary sun hangs constantly at zenith, there is no way to compute time; and so there is no such thing as time. I have come to believe that this is really true, because neither Perry nor I show any physical evidence of the passage of time. I was twenty when the iron mole broke through the crust of Pellucidar, and I don't look nor feel a great deal older now.

When I reminded Perry that he was one hundred and one years old, he nearly threw a fit. He said it was perfectly ridiculous and that Jason Gridley must have been hoaxing me; then he brightened up and called my attention to the fact that I was fifty-six. Fifty-six! Well, perhaps I should have been had I remained in Connecticut; but I'm still in my twenties down here.

When I look back at all that has happened to us at the Earth's core, I realize that a great deal more time has elapsed than has been apparent to us. We have seen so much. We have done so much. We have lived! We couldn't have crowded half of it into a lifetime on the outer crust. We have lived in the Stone Age, Perry and I—two men of the Twentieth Century—and we have brought some of the blessings of the Twentieth Century to these men of the Old Stone Age. They used to kill each other with stone hatchets and stone-shod spears before we came, and only a few tribes had even bows and arrows; but we have taught them how to make gunpowder and rifles and cannon, and they are commencing to realize the advantages of civilization.

I shall never forget, though, Perry's first experiments with gunpowder. When he got it perfected he was so proud you couldn't hold him. "Look at it!" he cried, as he exhibited a quantity of it for my inspection. "Feel of it. Smell of it. Taste it. This is the proudest day of my life, David. This is the first step toward civilization, and a long one."

Well, it certainly did seem to have all the physical attributes of gunpowder; but it must have lacked some of its spirit, for it wouldn't burn. Outside of that it was pretty good gunpowder. Perry was crushed; but he kept on experimenting, and after a while he produced an article that would kill anybody.

And then there was the beginning of the battle fleet. Perry and I built the first ship on the shores of a nameless sea. It was a flat-bottom contraption that bore a startling resemblance to an enormous coffin. Perry is a scientist. He had never built a ship and knew nothing about ship design; but he contended that because he was a scientist, and therefore a highly intelligent man, he was fitted to tackle the problem from a scientific basis. We built it on rollers, and when it was finished we started it down the beach toward the water. It sailed out magnificently for a couple of hundred feet and then turned over. Once again Perry was crushed; but he kept doggedly at it, and eventually we achieved a navy of sailing ships that permitted us to dominate the seas of our little corner of this great, mysterious inner world, and spread civilization and sudden death to an extent that amazed the natives. When I left Sari on this expedition I am about to tell you of, Perry was trying to perfect poison gas. He claimed that it would do even more to bring civilization to the Old Stone Age.

⋛ 2 ⋚

T H E natives of Pellucidar are endowed with a homing instinct that verges on the miraculous, and believe me they need it, for no man could find his way
anywhere here if he were transported beyond sight
of a familiar landmark unless he possessed this instinct; and this is quite understandable when you
visualize a world with a stationary sun hanging always at zenith, a world where there are neither moon
nor stars to guide the traveler—a world where because of these things there is no north, nor south, nor
east, nor west. It was this homing instinct of my
companions that led me into the adventures I am
about to narrate.

When we set out from Sari to search for von Horst, we followed vague clews that led us hither and yon from one country to another until finally we reached Lo-har and found our man; but returning to Sari it was not necessary to retrace our devious way. Instead, we moved in as nearly a direct line as possible, detouring only where natural obstacles seemed insurmountable.

It was a new world to all of us and, as usual, I found it extremely thrilling to view for the first time these virgin scenes that, perhaps, no human eye had ever looked upon before. This was adventure at its most glorious pinnacle. My whole being was stirred by the spirit of the pioneer and the explorer.

But how unlike my first experiences in Pellucidar, when Perry and I wandered aimlessly and alone in this savage world of colossal beasts, of hideous reptiles and of savage men. Now I was accompanied by a band of my own Sarians armed with rifles fabricated under Perry's direction in the arsenal that he had built in the land of Sari near the shore of the Lural Az. Even the mighty ryth, the monstrous cave bear that once roamed the prehistoric outer crust, held no terrors for us; while the largest of the dinosaurs proved no match against our bullets.

We made long marches after leaving Lo-har, sleeping quite a number of times, which is the only way by which time may be even approximately measured, without encountering a single human be-ing. The land across which we traveled was a para-dise peopled only by wild beasts. Great herds of antelope, red deer, and the mighty Bos roamed fer-tile plains or lay in the cool shade of the park-like forests. We saw the mighty mammoth and huge Maj, the mastadon; and, naturally, where there was so much flesh, there were the flesh-eaters—the tarag, the mighty sabre-tooth tiger; the great cave lions, and various types of carnivorous dinosaurs. It was an ideal hunters' paradise; but there were only beasts there to hunt other beasts. Man had not yet come to bring discord to this living idyl.

These beasts were absolutely unafraid of us; but they were inordinately curious, and occasionally we were surrounded by such great numbers of them as to threaten our safety. These, of course, were all herbivorous animals. The flesh-eaters avoided us when their bellies were full; but they were always dangerous at all times.

After we crossed this great plain we entered a forest beyond which we could see mountains in the far distance. We slept twice in the forest, and then came into a valley down which ran a wide river which flowed out of the foothills of the mountains we had seen.

The great river flowed sluggishly past us down toward some unknown sea; and as it was necessary to cross it I set my men at work building rafts.

These Pellucidarian rivers, especially the large ones with a sluggish current, are extremely dangerous to cross because they are peopled more often than not by hideous, carnivorous reptiles, such as have been long extinct upon the outer crust. Many of these are large enough to have easily wrecked our raft; and so we kept a close watch upon the surface of the water as we poled our crude craft toward the opposite shore.

It was because our attention was thus focused that we did not notice the approach of several canoes loaded with warriors, coming downstream toward us from the foothills, until one of my men discovered them and gave the alarm when they were only a matter of a couple of hundred yards from us.

I hoped that they would prove friendly, as I had no desire to kill them, for, primitively armed as they were, they would be helpless in the face of our rifles; and so I gave the sign of peace, hoping to see it acknowledged in kind upon their part; but they made no response.

Closer and closer they came, until I could see them quite plainly. They were heavy-built, stocky warriors with bushy beards, a rather uncommon sight in Pellucidar where most of the pure-blood white tribes are beardless.

When they were about a hundred feet from us, their canoes all abreast, a number of warriors rose in the bow of each boat and opened fire upon us.

I say, "opened fire," from force of habit. As a matter of fact what they did was to project dart-like missiles at us from heavy sling-shots. Some of my men went down, and immediately I gave the order to fire.

I could see by their manner how astonished the

bearded warriors were at the sound and effect of the rifles; but I will say for them that they were mighty courageous, for though the sound and the smoke must have been terrifying they never hesitated, but came on toward us even more rapidly. Then they did something that I had never seen done before nor since in the inner world. They lighted torches, made of what I afterward learned to be a resinous reed, and hurled them among us.

These torches gave off volumes of acrid black smoke that blinded and choked us. By the effects that the smoke had upon me, I know what it must have had upon my men; but I can only speak for myself, because, blinded and choking, I was helpless. I could not see the enemy, and so I could not fire at them in self-defense. I wanted to jump into the river and escape the smoke; but I knew that if I did that I should be immediately devoured by the ferocious creatures lurking beneath the surface.

I felt myself losing consciousness, and then hands seized me, and I knew that I was being dragged somewhere just as consciousness left me.

When I regained consciousness, I found myself

lying bound in the bottom of a canoe among the hairy legs of the warriors who had captured me. Above me, and rather close on either hand, I could see rocky cliffs; so I knew that we were paddling through a narrow gorge. I tried to sit up; but one of the warriors kicked me in the face with a sandaled foot and pushed me down again.

They were discussing the battle in loud, gruff voices, shouting back and forth the length of the boat as first one and then another sought to make himself heard and express his individual theory as to the strange weapon that shot fire and smoke with a thunderous noise and dealt death at a great distance. I could easily understand them, as they spoke the language that is common to all human beings in Pellucidar, insofar as I know, for I have never heard another. Why all races and tribes, no matter how far separated, speak this one language, I do not know. It has always been a mystery to both Perry and myself.

Perry suggests that it may be a basic, primitive language that people living in the same environment with identical problems and surroundings would naturally develop to express their thoughts. Perhaps he is right—I do not know; but it is as good an explanation as any.

They kept on arguing about our weapons, and getting nowhere, until finally the warrior who had kicked me in the face said, "The prisoner has got his senses back. He can tell us how sticks can be made to give forth smoke and flame and kill warriors a long way off."

"We can make him give us the secret," said another, "and then we can kill all the warriors of Gef and Julok and take all their men for ourselves."

I was a little puzzled by that remark, for it seemed to me that if they killed all the warriors there would be no men left; and then, as I looked more closely at my bearded, hairy captors, the strange, the astounding truth suddenly dawned upon me. These warriors were not men; they were women.

"Who wants any more men?" said another. "I don't. Those that I have give me enough trouble— gossiping, nagging, never doing their work properly. After a hard day hunting or fighting, I get all worn out beating them after I get home."

"The trouble with you, Rhump," said a third, "you're too easy with your men. You let them run all over you."

Rhump was the lady who had kicked me in the face. She may have been a soft-hearted creature; but she didn't impress me as such from my brief acquaintance with her. She had legs like a pro-football guard, and ears like a cannoneer. I couldn't imagine her letting anyone get away with anything because of a soft heart.

"Well," she replied, "all I can say, Fooge, is that if I had such a mean-spirited set of weaklings as your men are, I might not have as much trouble; but I like a little spirit in my men."

"Don't say anything about my men," shouted Fooge, as she aimed a blow at Rhump's head with a paddle.

Rhump dodged, and sat up in the boat reaching for her sling-shot, when a stentorian voice from the stern of the canoe shouted, "Sit down, and shut up."

I looked in the direction of the voice to see a perfectly enormous brute of a creature with a bushy black beard and close-set eyes. One look at her explained why the disturbance ceased immediately and Rhump and Fooge settled back on their thwarts. She was Gluck, the chief; and I can well imagine that she might have gained her position by her prowess.

Gluck fixed her bloodshot eyes upon me. "What is your name?" she bellowed.

"David," I replied.

"Where are you from?"

"From the land of Sari."

"How do you make sticks kill with smoke and a loud noise?" she demanded.

From what I had heard of their previous conversation, I knew that the question would eventually be forthcoming; and I had my answer ready for I knew that they could never understand a true explanation of rifles and gunpowder. "It is done by magic known only to the men of Sari," I replied.

"Hand him your paddle, Rhump," ordered Gluck.

As I took the paddle, I thought that she was going to make me help propel the canoe; but that was not in her mind at all.

"Now," she said, "use your magic to make smoke

and a loud noise come from that stick; but see that you do not kill anybody."

"It is the wrong kind of a stick," I said. "I can do nothing with it;" and handed it back to Rhump.

"What kind of a stick is it, then?" she demanded.

"It is a very strong reed that grows only in Sari," I replied.

"I think you are lying to me. After we get to Oog, you had better find some of those sticks, if you know what's good for you."

As they paddled up through the narrow gorge, they got to discussing me. I may say that they were quite unreserved in their comments. The concensus of opinion seemed to be that I was too feminine to measure up to their ideal of what a man should be.

"Look at his arms and legs," said Fooge. "He's muscled like a woman."

"No sex appeal at all," commented Rhump.

"Well, we can put him to work with the other slaves," said Gluck. "He might even help with the fighting if the village is raided."

Fooge nodded. "That's about all he'll be good for."

Presently we came out of the gorge into a large

valley where I could see open plains and forests, and on the right bank of the river a village. This was the village of Oog, our destination, the village of which Gluck was the chief.

⪎ 3 ⪏

O O G was a primitive village. The walls of the huts were built of a bamboo-like reed set upright in the ground and interwoven with a long, tough grass. The roofs were covered with many layers of large leaves. In the center of the village was Gluck's hut, which was larger than the others which surrounded it in a rude circle. There was no palisade and no means of defense. Like their village, these people were utterly primitive, their culture being of an extremely low order. They fabricated a few earthenware vessels, which bore no sort of decoration, and wove a few very crude baskets. Their finest craftsmanship went into the building of their canoes, but even these were very crude affairs. Their slingshots were of the simplest kind. They had a few stone axes and knives, which were considered treasures; and as I never saw any being fabricated while I was among these people, I am of the opinion that they were taken from prisoners who hailed from countries outside the valley. Their smoke-sticks were evidently their own invention, for I have never seen them elsewhere; yet I wonder how much better I could have done with the means at their command.

Perry and I used often to discuss the helplessness of twentieth-century man when thrown upon his own resources. We touch a button and we have light, and think nothing of it; but how many of us could build a generator to produce that light? We ride on trains as a matter of course; but how many of us could build a steam engine? How many of us could make paper, or ink, or the thousand-and-one little commonplace things we use every day? Could you refine ore, even if you could recognize it when you found it? Could you even make a stone knife with no more tools at your command than those possessed by the men of the Old Stone Age, which consisted of nothing but their hands and other stones?

If you think the first steam engine was a marvel of ingenuity, how much more ingenuity must it have taken to conceive and make the first stone knife.

Do not look down with condescension upon the men of the Old Stone Age, for their culture, by comparison with what had gone before, was greater than yours. Consider, for example, what marvelous inventive genius must have been his who first conceived the idea and then successfully created fire by artificial means. That nameless creature of a forgotten age was greater than Edison.

As our canoe approached the river bank opposite the village, I was unbound; and when we touched I was yanked roughly ashore. The other canoes followed us and were pulled up out of the water. A number of warriors had come down to greet us, and behind them huddled the men and the children, all a little fearful it seemed of the blustering women warriors.

I aroused only a mild curiosity. The women who

had not seen me before looked upon me rather contemptuously.

"Whose is he?" asked one. "He's not much of a prize for a whole day's expedition."

"He's mine," said Gluck. "I know he can fight, because I've seen him; and he ought to be able to work as well as a woman; he's husky enough."

"You can have him," said the other. "I wouldn't give him room in my hut."

Gluck turned toward the men. "Glula," she called, "come and get this. Its name is David. It will work in the field. See that it has food, and see that it works."

A hairless, effeminate little man came forward. "Yes, Gluck," he said in a thin voice, "I will see that he works."

I followed Glula toward the village; and as we passed among the other men and children, three of the former and three children followed along with us, all eying me rather contemptuously.

"These are Rumla, Foola and Geela," said Glula; "and these are Gluck's children."

"You don't look much like a man," said Rumla;

"but then neither do any of the other men that we capture outside of the valley. It must be a strange world out there, where the men look like women and the women look like men; but it must be very wonderful to be bigger and stronger than your women."

"Yes," said Geela. "If I were bigger and stronger than Gluck, I'd beat her with a stick every time I saw her."

"So would I," said Glula. "I'd like to kill the big beast."

"You don't seem very fond of Gluck," I said.

"Did you ever see a man who was fond of a woman?" demanded Foola. "We hate the brutes."

"Why don't you do something about it, then?" I asked.

"What can we do?" he demanded. "What can we poor men do against them? If we even talk back to them, they beat us."

They took me to Gluck's hut, and Glula pointed out a spot just inside the door. "You can make your bed there," he said. It seemed that the choice locations were at the far end of the hut away from the door, and the reason for this, I learned later, was that the men were all afraid to sleep near the door for fear raiders would come and steal them. They knew what their trials and burdens were in Oog; but they didn't know but what they might be worse off in either Gef or Julok, the other two villages of the valley, which, with the village of Oog, were always warring upon one another, raiding for men and slaves.

The beds in the hut were merely heaps of grass; and Glula went with me and helped me gather some for my own bed. Then he took me just outside the village and showed me Gluck's garden patch. Another man was working in it. He was an upstanding looking chap, evidently a prisoner from outside the valley. He was hoeing with a sharpened stick. Glula handed me a similar crude tool, and set me to work beside the other slave. Then he returned to the village.

After he was gone, my companion turned to me, "My name is Zor," he said.

"And mine is David," I replied. "I am from Sari."

" 'Sari.' I have heard of it. It lies beside the Lural Az. I am from Zoram."

"I have heard much of Zoram," I said. "It lies in the Mountains of the Thipdars."

"From whom have you heard of Zoram?" he asked.

"From Jana, the Red Flower of Zoram," I replied, "and from Thoar, her brother."

"Thoar is my good friend," said Zor. "Jana went away to another world with her man."

"You have slept here many times?" I asked.

"Many times," he replied.

"And there is no escape?"

"They watch us very closely. There are always sentries around the village, for they never know when they may expect a raid, and these sentries watch us also."

"Sentries or no sentries," I said, "I don't intend staying here the rest of my natural life. Some time an opportunity must come when we might escape."

The other shrugged. "Perhaps," he said; "but I doubt it. However, if it ever does, I am with you."

"Good. We'll both be on the lookout for it. We should keep together as much as possible; sleep at the same time, so that we may be awake at the same time. To what woman do you belong?"

"To Rhump. She's a she-jalok, if there ever was one; and you?"

"I belong to Gluck."

"She's worse. Keep out of the hut as much as you can, when she's in it. Do your sleeping while she's away hunting or raiding. She seems to think that slaves don't need any sleep. If she ever finds you asleep, she'll kick and beat you to within an inch of your life."

"Sweet character," I commented.

"They are all pretty much alike," replied Zor. "They have none of the natural sensibilities of women and only the characteristics of the lowest and most brutal types of men."

"How about their men?" I asked.

"Oh, they're a decent lot; but scared of their lives. Before you've been here long, you'll realize that they have a right to be."

We had been working while we talked, for the eyes of the sentries were almost constantly upon us. These sentries were posted around the village so that no part of it was left open to a surprise attack; and, likewise, all of the slaves were constantly under observation as they worked in the gardens. These warrior-women sentries were hard taskmasters, permitting no relaxation from the steady grind of hoeing and weeding. If a slave wished to go to his master's hut and sleep, he must first obtain permission from one of the sentries; and more often than not it was refused.

I do not know how long I worked in the gardens of Gluck the Chief. I was not permitted enough sleep; and so I was always half dead from fatigue. The food was coarse and poor, and was rationed to us slaves none too bountifully.

Half starved, I once picked up a tuber which I had unearthed while hoeing; and, turning my back on the nearest sentry, commenced to gnaw upon it. Notwithstanding my efforts of concealment, however, the creature saw me, and came lumbering forward. She grabbed the tuber from me and stuck it into her own great mouth, and then she aimed a blow at me that would have put me down for the count had it landed; but it didn't. I ducked under it. That made her furious, and she aimed another at me. Again I made her miss; and by this time she was livid with rage and whooping like an Apache, applying to me all sorts of vile Pellucidarian epithets.

She was making so much noise that she attracted the attention of the other sentries and the women in the village. Suddenly she drew her bone knife and came for me with murder in her eye. Up to this time I had simply been trying to avoid her blows for Zor had told me that to attack one of these women would probably mean certain death; but now it was different. She was evidently intent upon killing me, and I had to do something about it.

Like most of her kind, she was awkward, muscle-bound and slow; and she telegraphed every move that she was going to make; so I had no trouble in eluding her when she struck at me; but this time I did not let it go at that. Instead I swung my right to her jaw with everything that I had behind it, and she went down and out as cold as a cucumber.

"You'd better run," whispered Zor. "Of course you can't escape; but at least you can try, and you'll surely be killed if you remain here."

I took a quick look around, in order to judge what my chances of escape might be. They were nil. The women running from the village were almost upon me. They could have brought me down with their slingshots long before I could have gotten out of range; so I stood there waiting, as the women lumbered up; and when I saw that Gluck was in the lead I realized that the outlook was rather bleak.

The woman I had felled had regained consciousness and was coming to her feet, still a little groggy, as Gluck stopped before us and demanded an explanation.

"I was eating a tuber," I explained, "when this woman came and took it away from me and tried to beat me up. When I eluded her blows she lost her temper, and tried to kill me."

Gluck turned to the woman I had knocked down. "You tried to beat one of my men?" she demanded.

"He stole food from the garden," replied the woman.

"It doesn't make any difference what he did," growled Gluck. "Nobody can beat one of my men, and get away with it. If I want them beaten, I'll beat them myself. Perhaps this will teach you to leave my men alone," and with that she hauled off and knocked the other down. Then she stepped closer and commenced to kick the prostrate woman in the stomach and face.

The latter, whose name was Gung, seized one of Gluck's feet and tripped her. Then followed one of the most brutal fights I have ever witnessed. They pounded, kicked, clawed, scratched and bit one another like two furies. The brutality of it sickened me. If these women were the result of taking women out of slavery and attempting to raise them to equality with man, then I think that they and the world would be better off if they were returned to slavery. One of the sexes must rule; and man seems temperamentally better fitted for the job than woman. Certainly if full power over man has resulted in debauching and brutalizing women to such an extent, then we should see that they remain always subservient to man, whose overlordship is, more often than not, tempered by gentleness and sympathy.

The battle continued for some time, first one being on top and then another. Gung had known from the first that it was either her life or Gluck's; and so she fought with the fury of a cornered beast.

I shall not further describe this degrading spectacle. Suffice it to say that Gung really never had a chance against the powerful, brutal Gluck; and presently she lay dead.

Gluck, certain that her antagonist was dead, rose to her feet and faced me. "You are the cause of this," she said. "Gung was a good warrior and a fine hunter; and now she is dead. No man is worth that. I should have let her kill you; but I'll remedy that mistake." She turned to Zor. "Get me some sticks, slave," she commanded.

"What are you going to do?" I asked.

"I am going to beat you to death."

"You're a fool, Gluck," I said. "If you had any brains, you would know that the whole fault is yours. You do not let your slaves have enough sleep; you overwork them, and you starve them; and then you think that they should be beaten and killed because they steal food or fight in self-defense. Let them sleep and eat more; and you'll get more work out of them."

"What you think isn't going to make much difference after I get through with you," growled Gluck.

Presently Zor returned with a bundle of sticks from among which Gluck selected a heavy one and came toward me. Possibly I am no Samson; but neither am I any weakling, and I may say without boasting that one cannot survive the dangers and vicissitudes of the Stone Age for thirty-six years, unless he is capable of looking after himself at all times. My strenuous life here has developed a physique that was already pretty nearly tops when I left the outer crust; and in addition to this, I had brought with me a few tricks that the men of the Old Stone Age had never heard of, nor the women either; so when Gluck came for me I eluded her first blow and, seizing her wrist in both hands, turned quickly and threw her completely over my head. She landed heavily on one shoulder but was up again and coming for me almost immediately, so mad that she was practically foaming at the mouth.

As I had thrown her, she had dropped the stick with which she had intended to beat me to death. I stooped and recovered it; and before she could reach me, I swung a terrific blow that landed squarely on top of her cranium. Down she went—down and out.

The other women-warriors looked on in amazement for a moment; then one of them came for me, and several others closed in. I didn't need the evidence of the Stone Age invectives they were hurling at me, to know that they were pretty sore; and I realized that my chances were mighty slim; in fact they were nil against such odds. I had to do some very quick thinking right then.

"Wait," I said, backing away from them, "you have just seen what Gluck does to women who abuse her men. If you know what's good for you, you'll wait until she comes to."

Well, that sort of made them hesitate; and presently they turned their attention from me to Gluck. She was laid out so cold that I didn't know but that I had killed her; but presently she commenced to move, and after awhile she sat up. She looked around in a daze for a moment or two, and then her eyes alighted on me. The sight of me seemed to recall to her mind what had just transpired. She came slowly to her feet and faced me. I stood ready and waiting, still grasping the stick. All eyes were upon us; but no one moved or said anything; and then at last Gluck spoke.

"You should have been a woman," she said; and then, turning, she started back toward the village.

"Aren't you going to kill him?" demanded Fooge.

"I have just killed one good warrior; I am not going to kill a better one," snapped Gluck. "When there is fighting, he will fight with the women."

When they had all left, Zor and I resumed our work in the garden. Presently Gung's men came and dragged her corpse down to the river, where they rolled it in. Burial is a simple matter in Oog, and the funeral rites are without ostentation. Morticians and florists would starve to death in Oog.

It was all quite practical. There was no hysteria. The fathers of her children simply dragged her along by her hairy legs, laughing and gossiping and making ribald jests.

"That," I said to Zor, "must be the lowest and the saddest to which a human being can sink, that he go to his grave unmourned."

"You will be going down to the river yourself pretty soon," said Zor; "but I promise you that you'll have one mourner."

"What makes you think that I'll be going down to the river so soon?"

"Gluck will get you yet," he replied.

"I don't think so. I think Gluck's a pretty good sport, the way she took her beating."

" 'Good sport' nothing," he scoffed. "She'd have killed you the moment she came to, if she hadn't been afraid of you. She's a bully; and, like all bullies, she's a coward. Sometime when you're asleep, she'll sneak up on you and bash your brains out."

"You tell the nicest bedtime stories, Zor," I said.

⊰ 4 ⊱

OF COURSE the principal topic of conversation between Zor and me was for some time concerned with my set-to with Gluck, and prophesies on Zor's part that I was already as good as dead—just an animated corpse, in fact. But after I had slept twice, and nothing had happened to me, we drifted on to other topics and Zor told me how he happened to be so far from Zoram and what had led to his capture by the warrior-women of Oog.

Zor, it seemed, had been very much in love with a girl of Zoram, who one day wandered too far from the village and was picked up by a party of raiders from another country.

Zor immediately set out upon the trail of the abductors, which carried him through many strange
lands for what he estimated to have been a hundred
sleeps.

Of course it was impossible to know how far he
had travelled; but he must have covered an enormous
distance—perhaps two or three thousand miles; but
he never overtook the girl's abductors; and finally he
was captured by a tribe living in a palisaded village in
the heart of a great forest.

"I was there for many sleeps," he said, "my life
constantly in danger, for they were constanly threat-
ening to kill me to appease someone they called,
'Ogar.' Without any apparent reason at all, I quite
suddenly became an honored guest instead of a
prisoner. No explanation whatever was made to me.
I was allowed to go and come as I pleased; and,
naturally, at the first opportunity, I escaped. Inas-
much as there are several villages of these Jukans in
the forest, I hesitated to go on in that direction for
fear of being captured by some of the other villagers;
and so I climbed out of the valley with the intention
of making a wide detour; but after I came down out

of the mountains into this valley, I was captured."

"Where does the Valley of the Jukans lie?" I asked.

"There," he said, pointing in the direction of the snow-capped mountains that bordered one side of the valley.

"That, I think, is the direction I shall have to go to reach Sari," I said.

"You think?" he demanded. "Don't you know?"

I shook my head. "I haven't that peculiar instinct that the Pellucidarians have, which inevitably guides them toward their homes."

"That is strange," he said. "I can't imagine anyone not being able to go directly toward his home, no matter where he may be."

"Well, I am not a Pellucidarian, you see," I explained; "and so I have not that instinct."

"Not a Pellucidarian?" he demanded. "But there is nobody in the world who is not a Pellucidarian."

"There are other worlds than Pellucidar, Zor, even though you may never have heard of them; and I am from one of those other worlds. It lies directly beneath our feet, perhaps twenty sleeps distant."

He shook his head. "You are not, by any chance, a Jukan, are you?" he asked. "They, too, have many peculiar ideas."

I laughed. "No, I am not a Jukan," I asured him. And then I tried to explain to him about that other world on the outer crust; but, of course, it was quite beyond his powers of comprehension.

"I always thought you were from Sari," he said.

"I am, now. It is my adopted country."

"There was a girl from Sari among the Jukans," he said. "She was not a prisoner in the village where I was, but in another village a short distance away. I heard them talking about her. Some said they were going to kill her to appease Ogar. They were always doing something to appease this person Ogar, of whom they were terribly afraid; and then I heard that they were going to make her a queen. They were always changing their minds like that."

"What was the girl's name?" I asked.

"I never heard it," he said; "but I did hear that she was very beautiful. She is probably dead now, poor thing; but of course one can never tell about the Jukans. They may have made her a queen; they may have killed her; or they may have let her escape."

"By the way," I said, "what is the direction of Sari? You know, I was only guessing at it."

"You were right. If you were ever to escape, which you never will, you would have to cross those mountains there; and that would take you into the Valley of the Jukans; so you'd still be about as bad off as you are now. If I should ever escape, I'd have to go the same way in order to get on the trail of the people who stole Rana."

"Then we'll go together," I said.

Zor laughed. "When you get your mind set on anything, you never give up, do you?"

"I'll certainly not give up the idea of escaping," I told him.

"Well, it's nice to think about; but that's as far as we'll ever get with all these bewhiskered she-jaloks watching us every minute."

"An opportunity is bound to come," I said.

"In the meantime, look what else is coming!" he exclaimed, pointing up the valley.

I looked in the direction he indicated and saw a strange sight. Even as far away as they were, I recognized them as enormous birds upon which human beings were mounted.

"Those are the Juloks," said Zor; and at the same time he shouted to a sentry and pointed. Immediately the alarm was raised and our warrior-women came pouring out of the village. They carried knives and slingshots and the reeds which they fired to make their smoke-screen. About every tenth warrior carried a torch from which the others might light their reeds.

As Gluck came out of the village she tossed us each a knife and a slingshot, handed us smoke-reeds, and told us to join the women in the defense of the village.

We moved out in what might be described as a skirmish-line to meet the enemy, which was close enough now so that I could see them distinctly. The warriors were women, bushy-bearded and coarse like those of the Village of Oog; and their mounts were Dyals, huge birds closely resembling the Phororhacos, the Patagonian giant of the Miocene, remains of which have been found on the outer crust. They stand seven to eight feet in height, with heads larger than that of a horse and necks about the same thickness as those of horses. Three-toed feet terminate their long and powerful legs, which propel their heavy talons with sufficient force to fell an ox, while their large, powerful beaks render them a match for some of the most terrible of the carnivorous mammals and dinosaurs of the inner world. Having only rudimentary wings, they cannot fly; but their long legs permit them to cover the ground at amazing speed.

There were only about twenty of the Julok warrior-women. They came toward us slowly at first; and then, when about a hundred yards away, charged. Immediately our women lighted their torches and hurled them at the advancing enemy; and following this, they loosed their dart-like missiles upon the foe from their slingshots. Not all of the torches had been thrown at first, so that there were plenty in reserve as the enemy came closer to the blinding smoke. Now they were upon us; and I saw our women fighting like furies, with fearless and reckless abandon. They leaped into close quarters, trying to stab the Dyals or drag their riders from their backs.

The smoke was as bad for us, of course, as it was

"Quick," I cried, "Mount the thing!"

for the enemy; and I was soon almost helpless from choking and coughing. Zor was fighting beside me; but we were not much help to our cause, as neither of us was proficient in the use of the slingshot.

Presently, out of smothering smoke, came a riderless Dyal, the leather thong which formed its bridle dragging on the ground. Instantly, an inspiration seized me; and I grasped the bridle rein of the great bird.

"Quick!" I cried to Zor. "Perhaps this is the chance we have been waiting for. Mount the thing!"

He did not hesitate an instant, and, with my assistance, scrambled to the back of the great bird, which was confused and helpless by the smoke that it had inhaled. Then Zor gave me a hand up behind him.

We didn't know anything about controlling the creature, but we pulled its head around in the direction we wanted to go and then kicked its sides with our sandaled feet. It started slowly at first, groping its way through the smoke; but finally, when we came out where it was clearer and it sensed an opportunity to escape from the acrid fumes, it lit out like a scared rabbit; and it was with difficulty that Zor and I maintained our seats.

We headed straight for the mountains, on the other side of which lay the country of the Jukans, with little fear that our escape would be noticed until after the battle was over and the smoke had cleared away.

That was a ride! Nothing but another Dyal or an express train could have overtaken us. The creature was frightened and was really bolting. However, we were still able to guide it in the direction we wished to go. When we reached the foothills it was tired and was compelled to slow down, and after that we moved at a decorous pace up toward the higher mountains. And they were high! Snow-capped peaks loomed above us, an unusual sight in Pellucidar.

"This is an ideal way to cover ground," I said to Zor. "I have never travelled so rapidly in Pellucidar before. We are certainly fortunate to have captured this Dyal, and I hope that we can find food for him."

"If there's any question about that," replied Zor, "the Dyal will settle it himself."

"What do you mean?" I asked.

"He'll eat us."

Well, he didn't eat us; and we didn't keep him very long, for, as soon as we reached the snow, he positively refused to go any farther; and as he became quite belligerent we had to turn him loose.

≍ 5 ≍

T H E climate of Pellucidar is almost eternally Spring-like; and therefore the apparel of the inhabitants of this inner world is scant, being seldom more than a loin-cloth and sandals. The atmosphere near the surface is slightly denser than that of the outer crust because of centrifugence; but for the same reason it is much shallower than that of the exterior of the globe, with the result that it is extremely cold upon the heights of the higher mountains; so you may well imagine that Zor and I did not linger long in the snows of the upper levels.

He had crossed the mountains by this same pass when he had come out of the Valley of the Jukans;

so we were not delayed by the necessity for searching out a crossing.

The sun beat down upon us out of a clear sky; but it was still intensely cold, and in our almost naked state we could not have survived long. I can assure you that it was with a feeling of relief that we crossed the summit of the divide and started down the other slope. We were both numb with cold before we reached a warmer level.

The trail we followed had been made by game passing from one valley to another, and we were lucky that we met none of the carnivorous species while we were above the timber-line. Afterward, of course, we had the sanctuary of the trees into which to escape them. Our arms were most inadequate; for a stone knife is a poor weapon against a cave bear, the mighty ryth of the inner world, which stands eight feet at the shoulders and measures fully twelve feet in length, doubtless a perfect replica of *ursus spelaeus*, which roamed the outer crust contemporaneously with Paleolithic man. Nor were our slingshots much less futile, since we were far from proficient in their use.

Perhaps you can imagine how helpless one might feel, almost naked and practically unarmed, in this savage world. I often marvel that man survived at all, either here or upon the outer crust, he is by Nature so poorly equipped either for offense or defense. It is claimed that environment has a great deal to do with the development of species; and so it has always seemed strange to me, if this be true, that man is not fully as fleet of foot as the antelope, for in the environment in which he lived for ages he must have spent a great many of his waking hours running away from something—great beasts, which, not even by the wildest stretch of the imagination, could he have been supposed to have met and overcome with his bare hands, or even with a club or a knife. Personally, I feel that the human race must have developed in a wooded country where there was always a tree handy to offer man an avenue of escape from the terrible creatures that must have been constantly hunting him.

Well, we finally got down where it was warmer and where there were plenty of trees; and it was very fortunate for us, too, that there were trees, for the very first living creature that we met after negotiating the pass was a tarag, an enormous striped cat, the replica of which, our sabre-toothed tiger, has long been extinct upon the outer crust.

For large animals, they are extraordinarily fleet of foot; and they act so quickly when they sight their prey that unless an avenue of immediate escape is open or their intended victim is sufficiently well armed and alert, the result is a foregone conclusion— and the tarag feeds. Like all the other carnivorous animals of Pellucidar, they seem to be always hungry, their great carcasses requiring enormous quantities of food to rebuild the tissue wasted by their constant activity. They seem always to be roaming about. I do not recall ever having seen one of them lying down.

The tarag that we met, Zor and I chanced to see simultaneously, which was at the very instant that he saw us. He didn't pause an instant but charged immediately at unbelievable speed. Zor and I each voiced a warning and took to a tree.

I was directly in the path of the beast as it charged; and having its eye on me it leaped for me;

and it almost got me, too, its talons just scraping one of my sandals as it sprang high into the air after me.

Zor was in an adjoining tree and looked over at me and smiled. "That was a close call," he said. "We'll have to keep a better lookout."

"We'll have to have some weapons," I replied. "That is even more important."

"I'd like to know where you are going to get them," he said.

"I'll make them," I replied.

"What kind of weapons?"

"Oh, a couple of bows and some arrows, to start with, and two short, heavy hurling spears."

"What are bows and arrows?" he asked.

I explained them to him as well as I could; but he shook his head. "I'll make myself a spear," he said. "The men of Zoram kill even the ryth and the thipdar with the spear. That, and a knife are all the weapons I need."

After a while the tarag went away; and we came down to earth, and a little later we found a place to camp near a small stream. We were fortunate in not having to hunt very long for such a site, for places

It sprang high into the air after me

to camp in Pellucidar, which also mean places to sleep, must offer safety from prowling beasts of prey; and this means, ordinarily, nothing less than a cave the mouth of which can be barricaded.

It is a great world, this, and a great life; but eventually one becomes accustomed to being hunted. At first it used to keep my nerves constantly on edge; but after a while I took it just as casually as you of the outer world accept the jeopardies of traffic, hold-up men, and the other ordinary threats upon your life that civilization affords so abundantly.

We found a cave a couple of feet above high water in a cliff the face of which was washed by this mountain stream—a clear, cold stream in which we knew there would lurk no dangerous reptiles, a fact which was quite important to us since we had to wade into the stream to reach our cave. It was an ideal spot; and since neither of us had had sufficient sleep since being captured by the warrior-women of Oog, we were glad of the opportunity to lie up in safety until we were thoroughly rested.

After investigating the cave and finding it untenanted, dry, and large enough to accommodate us comfortably, we carried in leaves and dry grass for our beds, and were soon asleep.

How long I slept, I don't know. It may have been an hour or a week of your time; but the important thing was that when I awoke I was thoroughly rested. I may also add that I was ravenously hungry.

⊱ 6 ⊰

ONE seldom appreciates the little conveniences of everyday life until one is compelled to do without them. The chances are that you own a pocket knife, and that somewhere around the house or the garage there is a chisel and a saw, and perhaps a jack-plane and a hatchet and an axe; and it is also quite possible that, being a civilized man as you are, notwithstanding the fact that you have all these edged tools, you might have a devil of a time making a useable bow and the arrows to go with it, even though you had access to a lumber yard where you might select the proper materials cut more or less to the sizes you required. At the same time, you would have plenty of food in the pantry and the refrigerator; and there wouldn't be any large, inconsiderate beasts of prey lying in wait for you. The conditions would be ideal, and you could take all the time you required; but you would still have quite a job cut out for you. Consider then, your situation should you have at your disposal only a stone knife, your bare hands, and your materials on the hoof, as you might say. Add to this that you were hungry and that the filling of your belly depended largely upon the possession of a bow and arrow, to say nothing of the preservation of your life from the attacks of innumerable savage creatures which hungered for your flesh. This latter situation was the one in which I found myself after I awoke from my long sleep; but it really didn't give me undue concern, as I was by this time fully inured to the vicissitudes of life in the Stone Age.

Zor awoke shortly after I; and we went out together to search for materials for our weapons. We knew exactly what we wanted and it didn't take us long to find it in the lush vegetation of Pellucidar, notwithstanding the fact that hard woods are more or less scarce.

A species of the genus *Taxus* is more or less widely distributed throughout Pellucidar; and I had discovered that its wood made the best bows. For arrows I used a straight, hollow reed that becomes very hard when dry. The tips which I inserted in the end of the reeds were of wood, fire-hardened.

A modern archer of the civilized outer world would doubtless laugh at the crude bow I made then at the edge of the Valley of the Jukans. If he uses a yew bow, the wood for it was allowed to season for three years before it was made into a bow, and then the bow was probably not used for two more years; but I could not wait five years before eating; and so I hacked the limb I had selected from the tree with my stone knife and took the bark from it and tapered it crudely from the center toward each end. I prefer a six foot, eighty pound bow for a three-foot arrow, because of the great size and formidability of some of the beasts one meets here; but of course my bow did not attain this strength immediately. Every time we had a fire, I would dry it out a little more, so that it gradually attained its full efficiency. The strings for my bows I can make from several long-fibered plants; but even the best of them do not last long, and I am constantly having to renew them.

While I was making my bow and arrows, Zor fashioned a couple of the short, heavy spears such as are used by the warriors of Zoram. They are formidable weapons but only effective under a hundred feet, and only at that distance when hurled by a very powerful man; while my arrows can penetrate to the hearts of the largest beasts at a full hundred yards or more.

While we were working on our weapons we subsisted upon nuts and fruits; but as soon as they were completed we set out after meat; and this took us down into the valley, a large portion of which was thickly forested. We found the game a little wary, which suggested that it had been hunted; and therefore presupposed the presence of man. I finally made a very poor shot and succeeded only in wounding an antelope which made off into the forest, carrying my arrow with it. As I was quite sure that the wound would eventually bring it down, and as I have never liked to abandon a wounded animal and permit it to suffer, we followed the quarry into the forest.

The spoor was plain, for the trail was well marked with blood where the animal passed. Finally we caught up with it, and I dispatched it with another arrow through the heart.

I imagine that we relaxed our vigilance a little while we were cutting off a hind quarter and some of the other choice portions of our kill; for I certainly had no idea that we were not alone until I heard a man speak.

"Greetings," said a voice; and looking around I saw fully twenty warriors who had come from among the trees behind us.

"Jukans," whispered Zor.

There was that about their appearance which was rather startling. Their hair, which was rudely trimmed to a length of an inch or more, grew straight out from their scalps; but I think it was their eyes, more than any other feature, which gave them their strange appearance. As a rule, the iris was quite small and the whites of the eyeball showed all around it. Their mouths were flabby and loose, those of many of them constantly hanging open.

"Why do you hunt in our forest?" said he who had first spoken.

"Because we are hungry," I replied.

"You shall be fed then," he said. "Come with us to the village. You shall be welcome guests in the village of Meeza, our king."

From what Zor had told me of these people, I was not particularly anxious to go to one of their villages. We had hoped to skirt the forest in which their villages are located, and thus avoid them; but now it looked as though we were in for it after all.

"There is nothing that we would rather do," I said, "than visit your village; but we are in a great hurry, and we are going in the other direction."

"You are coming to our village," said the leader. His voice rose and cracked in sudden excitement, and I could see that even the suggestion had angered him.

"Yes," said several of the others, "you are coming to our village." They, too, seemed to be on the verge of losing control of themselves.

"Oh, of course," I said, "if you wish us to come, we shall be glad to; but we didn't want to put you to so much trouble."

"That is better," said the leader. "Now we shall all go to the village, and eat and be happy."

"I guess we're in for it," said Zor, as the warriors gathered around us and conducted us farther into the forest.

"They may continue to be friendly," he went on; "but one can never tell when their mood will change. All I can suggest is that we humor them as much as possible, for you saw the effect that even the slight suggestion of crossing them had upon them."

"Well, we won't cross them then," I said.

We marched for some little distance until we came at last to a crudely palisaded village that stood in a small clearing. The warriors at the gate recognized our escort and we were immediately admitted.

The village inside the palisade presented a strange appearance. It was evidently laid out according to no plan whatever, the houses having been placed according to the caprice of each individual builder. The result was most confusing, for there was no such thing as a street in the sense in which we understand it, for the spaces between the buildings could not be called streets. Sometimes they were only a couple of feet wide, and sometimes as much as twenty feet, and scarcely ever were they straight for more than the length of a couple of houses. The design of the houses was as capricious as their location, apparently no two of them having been built according to the same plan. Some were built of small logs; some of wattle and mud; some of bark; and there were many entirely of grass over a light framework. They were round, or square, or oblong, or conical. I noted one in particular that was a tower fully twenty feet high; while next to it was a woven grass hut that rose no more than three feet above the ground. It had a single opening, just large enough for its occupants to crawl in and out on their hands and knees.

In the narrow alleyways between the buildings, wild-eyed children played, women cooked, and men loafed; so it was with the greatest difficulty our escort forced its way toward the center of the village. We were constantly stepping over or around men, women or children, most of whom paid no attention to us, while others flew into frightful rages if we touched them.

We saw some strange sights during that short journey through the village. One man, sitting before his doorway, struck himself a terrific blow on the head with a rock. "Stop," he screamed, "or I'll kill you." "Oh you will, will you?" he answered himself, and then hit himself again; whereupon he dropped the rock and commenced to choke himself.

I do not know how his altercation with himself turned out, for we turned the corner of his house and lost sight of him.

A little farther on, we came upon a woman who was holding down a screaming child while she attempted to cut its throat with a stone knife. It was more than I could stand; and though I knew the risk I took, I seized her arm and pulled the knife from the child's throat.

"Why are you doing that?" I demanded.

"This child has never been sick," she replied; "and so I know there must be something the matter with it.

I am putting it out of its misery." Then, suddenly, her eyes ablaze, she leaped up and struck at me with her knife.

I warded off the blow, and simultaneously one of my escort knocked the woman down with the haft of his spear, while another pushed me roughly forward along the narrow alleyway. "Mind your own business," he screamed, "or you will get in trouble here."

"But you are not going to let the woman kill that child, are you?" I demanded.

"Why should I interfere with her? I might want to cut somebody's throat some day, myself; and I wouldn't want anyone to interfere with my fun. I might even want to cut yours."

"Not a bad idea," remarked another warrior.

We turned the corner of the house, and a moment later I heard the screams of the child again, but I was helpless to do anything about it, and now I had my own throat to think about.

Presently we came to a large open space below a low, rambling, crazy-looking structure. It was the palace of Meeza, the king. In the center of the plaza before the palace was a huge, grotesque, obscene figure representing a creature that was part man and part beast. Circling around it were a number of men turning "cartwheels." No one seemed to be paying any attention to them, although there were quite a number of people in the square.

As we passed the figure, each member of our escort said, "Greetings, Ogar!" and moved on toward the palace. They made Zor and me salute the hideous thing in the same manner.

"That is Ogar," said one of our escort. "You must always salute him when you pass. We are all the children of Ogar. We owe everything to him. He made us what we are. He gave us our great intelligence. He made us the most beautiful, the richest, the most powerful people in Pellucidar."

"Who are those men cavorting around him?" I asked.

"Those are the Priests of Ogar," replied the warrior.

"And what are they doing?" I asked.

"They are praying for the whole village," he replied. "They save us the trouble of praying. If they didn't pray for us, we'd have to; and praying is very strenuous and tiring."

"I should think it might be," I said.

We were admitted to the palace, which was as bizarre and mad a structure as I have ever seen; and there the leader of our escort turned us over to another Jukanian, a functionary of the palace.

"Here," he said, "are some very good friends who have come to visit Meeza and bring him presents. Do not, by any mischance, cut their throats, or permit anyone else to do so, lest they have difficulty in talking with Meeza, who is anxious, I know, to converse with them."

The palace functionary had been sitting on the floor when we entered, nor did he arise or discontinue his activities. Instead, he dismissed our escort and asked Zor and me to sit down and join him.

He had dug a hole in the dirt floor with the point of his knife, and into this hole he poured some water which he mixed with the loose earth he had excavated until the contents of the hole was of the consistency of soft modeling clay; then he took some in the palm of one hand, shaped it until it was round, patted it flat, and set it carefully on the floor beside him.

He inclined his head toward us and waved an inviting hand toward the hole. "Join me, please," he said. "You will find this not only exquisitely entertaining but highly enlightening and character building;" so Zor and I joined the palace functionary, and made mud pies.

⪥ 7 ⪤

GOOFO, the palace functionary in whose charge we had been placed, seemed quite pleased with us and our work. He told us that his undertaking was quite important, something of an engineering discovery that was going to revolutionize Pellucidar; and when he had finished telling us that, he shoved all the mud back into the hole, levelled it off, and patted it down with his hands until it was smooth on the surface like the rest of the floor.

"Well, well," he said, "that was a delicious meal. I hope you enjoyed it."

"What meal?" I blurted, for I was nearly famished. I hadn't eaten since I last slept.

He contracted his brows as though in an effort to recall something. "What were we doing?" he demanded.

"We were making mud pies," I said.

"Tut, tut," he said. "You have a very poor memory; but we will rectify that at once." He clapped his hands, then, and shouted something I did not understand; whereupon three girls entered from an adjoining apartment. "Bring food at once," demanded Goofo.

A short time later, the girls returned with platters of food. There were meat, vegetables, and fruit; and they certainly looked delicious. My mouth fairly watered in anticipation.

"Set it down," said Goofo; and the three girls placed the platters on the floor. "Now eat it," he said to them; and, dutifully, they fell to upon the food.

I moved a little closer to them and reached for a piece of meat; whereupon Goofo slapped my hand away and cried, "No, no."

He watched the girls very carefully as they consumed the food. "Eat it all," he said; "every bit of it;" and they did as he bid, while I sat gloomily watching my meal disappear.

When the girls had finished the meal, he ordered them from the room; and then turned to me with a sly wink. "I'm too smart for them," he said.

"Unquestionably," I agreed; "but I still don't understand why you made the girls eat our food."

"That's just the point. I wanted to discover if it were poisoned; now I know it wasn't."

"But I'm still hungry," I said.

"We'll soon rectify that," said Goofo; and again he clapped his hands and shouted.

Only one of the girls came in this time. She was a nice appearing, intelligent looking girl. Her expression was quite normal, but she looked very sad.

"My friends would sleep," said Goofo. "Show them to their sleeping quarters."

I started to say something, but Zor touched me on the arm. "Don't insist any longer on food," he said, guessing correctly what I had been on the point of saying. "It doesn't take much to upset these people, and then you can never tell what they will do. Right now, we are very fortunate that this Goofo is friendly."

"What are you two whispering about?" demanded Goofo.

"My friend was just wondering," I said, "if we were going to have the pleasure of being with you again after we have slept."

Goofo looked pleased. "Yes," he said; "but in the meantime, I want to put you on your guard. Just remember that there are a great many eccentric people in the village and that you must be very careful what you say and do. I, alone, am probably the only sane person here."

"I am glad you told us," I said; and then we followed the girl out of the apartment. In the next room, the other two girls were preparing food; and the sight and smell of it nearly drove me frantic.

"We have not eaten for a long time," I said to the girl who was accompanying us. "We are famished."

She nodded. "Help yourselves," she said.

"It won't get you in trouble?" I asked.

"No. Goofo has probably already forgotten that he has sent you to sleep. If he came in and saw you

eating, he would think that it was he who had suggested it; and these girls will forget almost as soon
as you are through that you have been here or that
you have eaten. They are little better than imbeciles.
In fact, everyone in the village is crazy except me."

I felt sorry for the poor thing, knowing that she
believed that she had impressed us with the truth of
her statement. I will admit that she didn't look crazy;
but it is one of the symptoms of insanity to believe
that everyone else is insane but you.

"What is your name?" I asked, as we sat down on
the floor, and commenced to eat.

"Kleeto," she said; "and yours?"

"David," I replied, "and my friend is Zor."

"Are you crazy, too?" she asked.

I shook my head and smiled. "No, indeed," I said.

"That's what they all say," she observed. She
caught herself suddenly, as though she had said something she should not have said, and quickly added,
"Of course I know you're not crazy, because I peeked
through the doorway and saw you working in the
mud with Goofo."

I wondered if she were ribbing me a bit, and then

"I will admit she did not look crazy."

I realized that to her poor unbalanced mind the thing that we had been doing might seem entirely natural and rational. With a sigh, I continued my meal—a sigh for the poor warped brain that dominated such a lovely girl.

Zor and I were famished; and Kleeto looked on in amazement at the amount of food we consumed. The two other girls paid no attention to us, but went on with their work preparing more food. At last we could eat no more; and Kleeto led us to a darkened room and left us to sleep.

I don't know how long we were in the palace of Meeza. I know we slept many times; and we lived off the fat of the land. Kleeto saw to that, for she seemed to have taken a liking to us. Nobody seemed to know what we were doing in the palace; but after they became accustomed to seeing us around, they paid no more attention to us, except that we were not permitted to leave the building, which meant, of course, that we could not escape; but we bided our time, hoping that some day something would occur to give us the opportunity for which we so longed.

Goofo, who was major-domo of the palace, never

could recall why we were there. I used to see him sitting with that puzzled look on his face gazing at us intently, and I knew perfectly well that he was trying to recall who we were and why we were in the palace.

As time went on, I became more and more impressed with Kleeto's intelligence. She had an excellent memory, and by comparison with the others that we met she was unquestionably sane. Zor and I used to like to talk with her whenever the opportunity arose. She told us much about the ways of the people and the gossip of the palace.

"Which village are you from?" she asked one day.

"Village? I don't understand," I said. "Zor is from the land of Zoram, and I am from the land of Sari."

She looked puzzled for a moment. "Do you mean to tell me that you are not Jukans from another village?" she demanded.

"Certainly not. What made you think we were?"

"Because Goofo said that you were his friends, and were to be treated well; so I was positive you were not prisoners and, therefore, must be Jukans from another village. I will admit, however, that I was puzzled, because you seemed to be far too intelligent to be Jukans. They, as you have doubtless discovered, are all maniacs."

A light commenced to dawn in my mind then. "Kleeto, you are not a Jukan?" I asked.

"Certainly not," she said. "I am a prisoner here. I come from the land of Suvi."

I had to laugh at that; and she asked me why I was laughing. "Because all the time, I thought you were crazy; and you thought we were crazy."

"I know it," she said. "It is very funny indeed; but after you have lived here awhile, you don't know who is crazy and who isn't. Some of the Jukans look and act perfectly normal; and they may be the craziest of the lot. Now neither Meeza, the king, nor Moko, his son, look like imbeciles; and, well, they are not exactly imbeciles either; but they are both maniacs of the worst type, irresponsible and cruel, always ready to kill."

"Goofo doesn't seem such a bad lot," I said.

"No, he's harmless. You were lucky to fall into his hands. If Noak, his assistant, had been on duty when

you were brought into the palace, it might have been
a very different story."

"You have been here a long while, Kleeto?" I asked.

"Yes, for more sleeps than I can count. In fact, I
have been here for so long that they have forgotten
that I am not one of them. They think I am a Jukan."

"It should be easy for you to escape, then," I suggested.

"It would do me no good to escape alone," she said.
"What chance would I have to reach Suvi, alone and
unarmed?"

"We might all go together," I said.

She shook her head. "There has never been a single opportunity, since I have been here, when three
people might have escaped from the palace, let alone
getting out of the village. There have been many
prisoners here, and I have never heard of one escaping. By the way," she added, "you said you were
from Sari, didn't you?"

"Yes," I replied.

"There is a prisoner here from Sari, a girl," she said.

"In this village?" I demanded. "I had heard that
there was a Sarian girl in one of the Jukan villages;

but I did not know that she was here. Do you know her name?"

"No," replied Kleeto, "and I have not even seen her; but I understand that she is very beautiful."

"Where is she?" I asked.

"Somewhere in the palace. The High Priest keeps her hidden. You see, Meeza wants to take her as one of his wives; Moko, his son, wants her; and the High Priest wants to sacrifice her to Ogar."

"Which of these will get her?" I asked.

"The High Priest already has her; but he is afraid of Meeza; and Meeza is afraid to take her away from the High Priest for fear of bringing down the wrath of Ogar on his head."

"So for the moment she is safe," I said.

"In the palace of Meeza, the king, no one is ever safe," replied Kleeto.

≍ 8 ≍

SLEEPING and eating constituted our principal activities in the palace of Meeza, the king. It was no life for a couple of warriors, and the boredom of it fairly drove us mad.

"We'll be as crazy as the rest of them, if we don't get out of here pretty soon," said Zor.

"I don't know what we're going to do about it," I said.

"Perhaps we can persuade Goofo to let us go out into the city," suggested Zor. "At least that would give us a little exercise and break the monotony of our life here."

"It might give us an opportunity to escape, as well," I said.

Zor arose, yawning, and stretched. He was getting fat and loggy. "Let's go find him."

As we were about to leave the chamber, we heard a scream—just a single scream, followed by silence.

"Now I wonder what that was?" said Zor.

"It was very close by," I said. "Perhaps we had better wait. You can never tell what trouble you may run into, if anything happens to excite these people; and it sounded to me as though that scream may have come from Goofo's office."

Presently Kleeto entered the room in what was evidently a state of excitement. "What's the matter?" I asked. "What makes you so nervous?"

"Did you hear the scream?" she asked.

"Yes."

"That was Goofo. Noak just stabbed him in the back."

Zor whistled.

"Did he kill him?" I demanded.

"I don't know; but it is very probable. At any rate, he is badly wounded; and Noak is major-domo of the palace. It will go hard with all of us now. Noak has more brains than Goofo, and a good memory. He won't forget all about us the way Goofo did."

"I don't think he's ever seen us," said Zor.

"That won't make any difference," said Kleeto. "He'll commence to investigate now and find out all about everybody in his part of the palace."

"It's too bad we aren't dressed like Jukans," I said; "then we might make Noak think we were visitors from another village."

The Jukans' loin-cloths were of monkey skin cured with the hair on; and they wore monkey-skin anklets and necklaces of human teeth; and, as I have mentioned before, their hair was cut quite short; so it would have been very difficult for us to pass as Jukans in our present state.

"Couldn't you find us each an outfit, Kleeto?" asked Zor.

"I know where there is one outfit," replied the girl. "It belonged to a man who used to serve under Goofo. He suddenly conceived the idea that he shouldn't wear any apparel at all; so he threw it away and went naked. All the things he discarded were put in one of the storerooms; and, as far as I know, they are still there."

"Well, let's hope he hasn't come back to get his things," said Zor.

"He hasn't," said Kleeto; "and he never will. He came naked into the presence of the king; and Meeza had him destroyed."

"Now if we could find another outfit," said Zor, "we might even get out of the palace without being noticed."

As we talked, I was standing facing the doorway, which was covered by hangings made from a number of softly tanned skins of some small animal. I saw the hanging move slightly; and, guessing that someone was eavesdropping, I stepped quickly to it and drew it aside. Beyond it stood a man with a foul face. His close-set, beady black eyes, his long nose and receding chin, gave him a rat-like appearance. He stood there looking at us for a moment in silence; then he turned and scurried away precisely like a rat.

"I wonder if he heard?" said Kleeto.

"Who was he?" asked Zor.

"That was Ro," replied the girl. "He is one of Noak's henchmen."

"It looks as though we are in for it," said Zor, "for he certainly must have heard us."

"Perhaps he'll forget all about us before he finds anyone to tell it to," I said.

"Not he," rejoined Kleeto. "Sometimes it seems as though the meaner they are, the better their memory."

"Now," I said, "would be a good time to get out of here, if we could disguise ourselves as Jukans. Suppose you get that one outfit, Kleeto, and we'll fix Zor up. If he can go around the palace, undetected, he may find an opportunity to get the things necessary to outfit me."

"But how about my hair?" demanded Zor.

"Can't you find us a knife, Kleeto?" I asked.

"Yes. We have a number of knives with which we prepare the food. I'll get you a couple of them right away."

After Kleeto got the knives, she left us to see if she could find the garments for Zor; and I set about cutting his hair, which had grown quite long. It was quite a job; but at last it was completed.

"Open your eyes wide and let your chin drop," I told him, laughingly, "and you might pass for a Jukan."

Zor made a wry face. "Come on," he said, "and I'll make an imbecile out of you now."

He had just about completed hacking off my hair, when Kleeto returned with a Jukan outfit.

"You'd better go into your sleeping quarters and change," she said. "Someone might come in here."

After Zor left the room, Kleeto returned to her work in the kitchen; and I was left alone. As usual, when I was alone, and my mind not occupied with futile plans to escape, my thoughts went back to Sari and to my mate, Dian the Beautiful. Doubtless she had given me up for lost; and if I never returned, my fate would remain a mystery to her and to my fellow Sarians.

Sari seemed a long way off; and in truth it was; and almost hopeless any thought that I might ever return; for even should I escape from the Jukans, how might I ever hope to find Sari, I who was not endowed with the homing instinct of the Pellucidarians?

Of course, Zor could point the general direction of Sari; but without him, or another Pellucidarian at my side, I might wander for a lifetime in a great circle; or even if I travelled in what I felt to be a straight line, the chances were very remote that I would ever hit upon the relatively tiny spot that is Sari. However, no doubts would deter me from making the attempt to escape should the opportunity ever be presented; nor should I ever cease to try to return to my Dian as long as life remained to me.

Thus was my mind occupied when the hangings of the doorway were thrust aside and a man strode into the apartment. He was a well muscled fellow; but his face was neither that of a man nor a beast. Stiff, upstanding hair grew almost to his eyes, so that he had no forehead whatsoever, or at least only a narrow strip above his brows about an inch wide. His eyes were so close-set as to seem almost one; and his ears were pointed like a beast's. His nose was not bad; but his lips were thin and cruel. He stood there looking at me in silence for a few moments, a sneer curling his lips.

"So," he said at last, "you are going to escape, are you?"

"Who are you?" I demanded.

"I am Noak, the major-domo of the palace of Meeza," he replied.

"So what?" I demanded. Everything about the fellow antagonized me; and I could tell from his attitude that he had come looking for trouble; so I made no effort to appease him. Whatever he intended doing, he was going to do no matter what I said or did; and I wanted to get it over with.

"You have even cut your hair so that you will look more like a Jukan. All you need now is a loin-cloth and ornaments of a Jukan, I suppose."

"That is all," I said, looking at his loin-cloth.

Suddenly his eyes blazed in maniacal fury. "So you thought you could escape from Noak, did you? Well, I'll fix you. You'll never escape from anybody, when I get through with you." And with that, he drew his stone knife and came for me.

Now, I had kept one of the knives that Kleeto had obtained for us; and Zor had retained the other; so I was not without some means of defense, and I was ready for him when he came.

I hope that you never have to fight with a madman. It is one of the most frightful experiences that I have ever passed through. Noak was not only mad, but he was a powerful man as well; but really the most harrowing part of the encounter was the horror of that bestial face, the mad light in those terrible eyes, the froth of rage upon those cruel lips, the bared, yellow fangs.

I parried his first blow and struck at his chest with my own weapon; but he partially avoided me, and I succeeded only in inflicting a slight flesh wound. Even this, however, goaded him into an increased fury of rage; and now he struck at me again at close quarters, at the same time clutching for my throat with his free hand. Once more I eluded him; and then, with a scream, he sprang into the air and lit full on top of me. I lost my balance then and toppled backward to the floor, with the maniac on top of me. He raised his knife to finish me; but I clutched his wrist and somehow succeeded in tearing the weapon from his grasp. Then he bared those yellow fangs and bit at me, seeking to fasten them upon my jugular.

I was forced to release his wrist then, to push him away from me; and I succeeded in getting my fingers at his throat. I still clung to my knife; and now as we strained and struggled in each other's grasp I got the point of it beneath his heart; and with all my strength I drove it home.

He screamed and struggled spasmodically for a few seconds; then he relaxed in death.

I pushed his body from me and staggered to my feet, half nauseated by the horror of the encounter and the nearness of that repulsive face to mine.

As I stood there panting for breath, I heard a sound at the doorway behind me. I wheeled about, ready for another enemy; but it was only Kleeto. She stood there, wide-eyed, looking at the corpse upon the floor.

"You have killed Noak," she said, in a half whisper.

"And I have the outfit of a Jukan," I replied.

⊱ 9 ⊰

BEFORE I came to Pellucidar, I had never killed a man. In fact, I had never seen anyone who had met a violent death; but since then I have killed many men, always, however, in self-defense or in defense of others. It must always have been thus, and must always be, in a society where there is no regularly constituted force of guardians of the peace and safety of man. Here, in Pellucidar, each man must be, to a great extent, his own police force, his own judge and jury. This does not mean that right always prevails; more often it is might; but where an individual has both right and might on his side, he feels a far greater personal satisfaction in his conquests than he possibly could by calling in a policeman and turning a malefactor over to the slow processes of the courts, where even right may not always prevail.

I presume that Kleeto had witnessed such deaths many times; and so it was not the killing of Noak that affected her, but rather the fear of what must happen to me if my crime were discovered.

"Now you are in for it," she said.

"There wasn't much of anything else I could do about it, was there?" I inquired; "unless I was content to let him kill me."

"I would never have thought that you could kill him. He was very powerful."

"Well, it's done now, and can't be undone; and the next problem is how to remove the evidence."

"We might bury it," she said. "There is no other way of hiding it."

"But where?" I asked.

"Your sleeping quarters," she said. "That would be the safest place."

A newly dead body is a difficult thing to handle before rigor mortis sets in, and for some reason it

seems about twice as heavy and four times as awkward as in life; but I managed to get Noak's body
across one of my shoulders and carry it into the sleeping quarters occupied by Zor and myself. Zor,
dressed like a Jukan, was just coming out as I approached with my burden.

"Now what!" he exclaimed.

"Noak tried to kill me," I said.

"That is Noak?" His tone was incredulous.

"It was," I replied.

"David had to kill him," said Kleeto; "and I think
it is just as well for all of us that Noak is dead."

"Why are you bringing him here?" asked Zor.

"I'm going to bury him in our sleeping quarters."

Zor scratched his head. "From the looks of him,
he'll be better company dead than alive. Come on,
bring him in and I'll help you dig."

We dug a narrow trench about three feet deep
near one of the walls of our sleeping chamber. Kleeto
got another knife from the kitchen and helped us; but
even with the three of us working it was rather a
slow process. We'd loosen up the hard-packed earth
of the floor with the points of our stone knives,

and then scoop the loose dirt out with our hands; but after awhile it was done, and we rolled Noak in and covered him up, tamping the earth down solidly all around him. The excess earth we spread evenly over the floor of the chamber and tramped it down as best we could. We placed some sleeping mats over the grave, and in the dim light of the room I am sure that nothing would have appeared amiss to anyone who might have come to investigate.

"Now," I said to Zor, after we had completed our labors, "let's get out of here."

"Where shall we go?" he asked.

"We should try to get out of the palace and into the city," I replied, "and we should do it right now before Noak is missed. Come on, Kleeto, you may get back to Suvi, after all."

"You're going to take me with you?" asked the girl in a tone of surprise.

"Surely. You're one of us, aren't you? Without your help, we wouldn't have had a chance."

"I'm afraid that having a woman along might make it difficult for you," she said. "You two had better go on alone. You might possibly get me out of the palace; but I doubt very much that you could pass me through the gates of the village."

"That remains to be seen," I said, "and anyway we won't go without you."

"Of course not," said Zor. "If they stop us at the gate, we'll tell them we're visitors from another village, on our way home."

"Tell them we're from Gamba," said Kleeto. "That is the farthest village. Few ever come from there to this village; so there is little likelihood that they could check up on us."

Well, we didn't even get out of the palace. The guard wouldn't let us pass without permission from Noak; and when we insisted, I saw that they were becoming suspicious, so I said, "All right, we'll go and get Noak."

We were very much disheartened as we retraced our steps, for now it seemed hopeless to even think of escape. We talked it over, and finally Zor and I came to the conclusion that the only hope we had was to familiarize ourselves with the palace on the chance that there might be some less well-guarded exit. There was just one ray of hope shining through our gloom. It was the fact that no one had suspected that we were not Jukans.

Kleeto said that she believed there was another way out of the palace, because she had heard that Meeza and Moko often went out into the city, and she was quite sure that they did not leave by the main entrance.

"I think that they have some secret way," she said.

"Zor and I will try to find it," I said. "You stay here; and if we find a way to escape, we'll come back and get you."

The palace of Meeza, the king, must have covered several acres of ground. It was a village in itself, and like the outer village its design followed the vagaries of a mad mind. There were turning, twisting, gloomy corridors that led nowhere, ending in a blank wall. There were pitch-dark rooms without windows, and many little courts that were in reality rooms without roofs. How the inmates found their way around is quite beyond me; and I did not see how we could find our way back to Kleeto, if we discovered an avenue of escape. I said as much to Zor; but he assured me that he could retrace our steps.

Evidently every foot of the way was indelibly
stamped upon his memory, the result of a faculty,
no doubt, that was definitely associated with his inherent homing instinct.

As we wandered through the palace, we were constantly meeting people; but no one seemed to suspect
us, with the result that we became over-confident
and very bold, prying into places where we had no
business to be, as we searched for the secret way
which we hoped would lead us to freedom. At last,
we became hungry and tired; and, as up to then we
had found no food, we decided to lie down and sleep;
so we curled up in a corner of a dark room and prayed
that food would be easy to find when we awoke.

Many of you who live upon the outer crust fear
the darkness that comes with night. You think of
it as the time that hunting beasts prowl and criminals
carry on their nefarious practices; but I can truth-
fully assure you that for twelve hours out of the
twenty-four, I would gladly trade the perpetual sun
of the inner world for the sheltering darkness of your
nights. Under the cover of darkness, we might have
found many opportunities to escape from the village

of Meeza. Under the beneficent shelter of darkness, we might have carried on our operations in safety not only because it was dark but because where night regularly follows day it is the time set apart for sleeping; and so there would have been but comparatively few eyes to detect us; but where there is no night, there is no regular time to sleep; and so at least half of the people are abroad at all times, or, what is more likely, two-thirds of them. So you can see that our chances of sneaking out, unnoticed, were extremely thin. Yes, I would have given a great deal for one good, dark night.

When we awoke, we continued our aimless search for the secret exit from the palace. We tried to do it systematically, following one corridor after another to its end. We found portions of the palace that seemed to have been untenanted for years and others crowded with Jukans so thickly that we passed among them unnoticed, protected by their very numbers.

Just as there seemed to be no plan to the palace, which covered several acres of ground, the activities of its inmates appeared equally aimless. We encoun-

tered all degrees of mental ineptitude, from harmless
halfwits to raving maniacs, from jibbering idiots to
men of apparently normal intelligence.

One man was running madly around in a small
circle. Another squatted cross-legged upon the floor,
staring at a spot on a wall a couple of feet in front
of him; while directly behind him a man was hacking
another to pieces with a stone hatchet, not even the
terrible screams of the victim attracting the attention
of the sitter. Two men and a woman looked on, apa-
thetically; but presently their attention was attracted
by a bushy-headed maniac, who came galloping
through the apartment on all fours, shrieking, "I'm a
ryth. I'm a ryth."

That was all right with them, too, until he attempted to prove that he was a ryth by biting one
of the men. The two were lying on the floor, biting
and clawing at one another, as Zor and I passed on
through the chamber in our interminable search.

We had slept three times since we had parted from
Kleeto, and had always managed to find sufficient
food, on a couple of occasions sitting down at meals

with idiots who seemed not even to notice our presence.

Once we had gone for some time without food and were both famished, when we came to a large room in which there was a long table where perhaps a hundred men were eating. As there were several vacant places at the table, we sauntered over and sat down, assuming that, as upon the other two occasions, no one would pay any attention to us; but we were very much mistaken. Sitting at the far end of the table was a man wearing a feather headdress. "Who are those two men?" he shouted, as we sat down. "I have never seen them before."

"I know who they are," cried a man sitting opposite us; and I looked up into the rat-like face of Ro.

"Well, who are they?" demanded the man with the headdress. "And what are they doing here at the king's table?"

"I do not know what they are doing at the king's table, Meeza," replied Ro; "but I know who they are. They were brought in to Goofo many, many sleeps ago; and they disappeared when Noak disappeared."

So we had by accident stumbled into the king's dining room; and the man with the feather headdress was Meeza. It certainly looked as though we might have to do some explaining.

"Well," cried Meeza, "who are you and what are you doing here?"

"We are visitors from Gamba," replied Zor.

"I think they are lying," said Ro. "The last time I saw them, they were not dressed like Jukans, but like strangers from another country."

"What are your names?" demanded Meeza. Although he had more than the usual amount of control for a Jukan, I could see that he was commencing to get excited. So unstable are they that the least little thing is apt to upset them; and after that there is no telling what will happen.

"My companion's name is Zor," I replied, "and mine is David."

" 'Zor,' " repeated Meeza. "That might be the name of a Jukan, but not David. Take that one and tie him up." Meeza was pointing at me. "Zor, you shall be a welcome guest in the palace of Meeza, the king."

"And what about David?" asked Zor.

"We need an offering to appease Ogar," replied Meeza, "and David will do very well. Take him away, men."

"But David is all right," insisted Zor. "He is my friend, and I know he is all right. You should not harm him, Meeza."

Meeza leaped to his feet, his eyes blazing in a frenzy of rage. "You dare disagree with me?" he screamed. "I should have your heart cut out," and then his voice dropped and he said in gentle tones, "But you are my honored friend. Come, eat and drink with us."

As I was being dragged away, I saw two servants come in bearing a huge mastadon tusk filled to the brim with some liquid. It was handed to Meeza, who drank from it, and then passed it to the man at his right. Thus, it started the rounds of the table as I was finally dragged from the room.

My escort wound through several corridors and finally led me into a small room, the doorway of which was closed with a crude gate which was held in place by wooden bars on the outside. Into this dimly lighted cell they shoved me, tied my hands behind my back, and left me.

The outlook was anything but rosy. Here I was, definitely a prisoner and condemned to be sacrificed to their heathenish god. The only ray of sunshine penetrating the bleak outlook emanated from the clumsy, crazy manner in which they had bound my hands behind me. Even while they were doing it, I felt that it would not be difficult to free myself; and this I succeeded in doing shortly after they had left me; but the barred gate that closed my cell defied my every effort to force it, and I was still a prisoner condemned to death.

⋊ IO ⋉

AS I LAY there in my dark cell, I found food for thought in these strange people into whose clutches Fate had thrust me. They were unquestionably maniacs and yet they had achieved a few more of the attributes of civilization than any of the native tribes of Pellucidar with which I was familiar. They lived in villages instead of caves; they sat at tables to eat instead of squatting on the bare ground; and they had a god whom they worshipped in the form of an idol.

I wondered what strange freak of Fate had rendered an entire nation mad, and whether future gen-

erations would become more violent or if the seed
of madness would eventually die out; and while I
was thinking of these things I fell asleep and dreamed
of Sari and Abner Perry and Dian the Beautiful, so
that when I awoke my heart was heavy with regret
that I could not have slept on, dreaming thus, forever.

When I awoke I was ravenously hungry, for,
though I had sat at the king's table, I had had no
chance to eat, so quickly had I been hustled out. I
wondered if they would bring me food, but knowing these people as I did I realized that they might
forget me entirely and that I might lie here until I
starved to death.

For want of something better to do, I thought I
would pace off the dimensions of my cell—anything
to keep my mind occupied. It was quite dark and
so I groped my way to one of the side walls and then
moved slowly toward the back of the cell, keeping
one hand upon the wall. I was surprised that what
I had first thought to be a small room should be so
large. In fact, it proved perfectly enormous. Fi-

nally the truth dawned upon me. They had locked me up in a corridor.

I crossed it and found that it was only a couple of paces in width. Where did it lead? I determined to follow it and find out; but first I returned to the wall against which I had started, so that, by keeping my hand constantly against that wall, I could always return to the part from which I had started, if I so desired. This precaution was quite necessary for the reason that there might be branching corridors or cross corridors that I might miss in the darkness did I not keep one hand constantly upon the same wall.

Like all the other corridors I had seen, this one ran first in one direction and then another; but always it ran through utter darkness.

I had been following the passageway for some time when I heard voices ahead of me. They were faint and muffled at first; but as I continued to grope my way along they became plainer; so I knew that I was approaching them. At last I could make them out. They were the voices of a man and a woman.

They seemed to be arguing about something, and presently I could hear their words.

"If you will come away with me, I will take you back to your own country," said the man. "If you remain here, Bruma will sacrifice you to Ogar. Not even Meeza could save you, although he would like to have you for himself."

"I do not believe you," said a woman's voice, "because you know you could never get me out of the city. As soon as I was missed, Bruma and Meeza would have the city searched."

"Little good would it do them," said the man, "for we should be well out of the city before anyone knew that we had gone. Right here is a corridor that leads to a cave in the forest beyond the walls of the village, right here behind this door." And with that, he struck a panel of wood with his knuckles so close to my ear that it made me jump.

So this was the corridor leading out of the palace. The poor crazy halfwits had locked me into the only avenue by which I could escape. It was very amusing. How I wished that Kleeto and Zor were with me. It would be quite futile to attempt to return for them now. In the first place I couldn't have gotten out of the corridor into the palace, and if I had been able to do so how was I to reach Zor, who was now an honored guest of Meeza. I should certainly have been recognized had I gone prowling around the king's quarters looking for my friend, nor could I have found my way to Kleeto along the devious passageways of the palace. Still, I hated to abandon my friends; and so I stood there in the darkness trying to conjure some plan out of the thin air whereby I might get word to Zor and Kleeto.

As I stood there thinking, I could hear the man beyond the partition speaking in low tones to the woman; but his voice did not carry his words to me until presently he raised it.

"I tell you that I love you," he said, "and Meeza or no Meeza, Bruma or no Bruma, I am going to have you."

"I already have a mate," replied the woman; "and if I didn't, I would as soon mate with a jalok as you."

"You compare me with a jalok, slave!" cried the man, his voice rising in anger. "I, Moko, the king's son! You dare insult me!"

"It was the jalok I insulted," said the woman.

"By Ogar!" screamed the man, "no one shall have you now, nor shall you ever see Sari again. For this insult, slave, you die."

So this was the girl from Sari. I waited to hear no more, but hurled myself against the panel in front of me. It crashed inward beneath my weight; and I stepped into a room to see a girl in the clutches of Moko, the son of Meeza. The girl's back was toward me, but over her shoulder the man saw me. His eyes were blazing with maniacal fury as he sought to free the hand in which he held his knife from the grasp of his intended victim.

"Get out of here," he screamed at me. "Get out!"

"Not until I am done with you," I said, as I advanced toward him, stone knife in hand.

"I am Moko," he said, "the king's son. I tell you to get out. Disobey me, and you die."

"It is not I who am going to die," I said, as I closed on him.

With a scream, he pushed the girl from him and came for me. He was far more skilled in the use of a knife than I; and had I depended solely upon that

As he went by I plunged my knife between his ribs

weapon, I should have died there in the palace of Meeza, the king. But I didn't depend upon my knife and I didn't die. I parried his first blow with my right forearm and crossed with my left to his chin. He went down to that blow but was up again almost immediately and coming for me again, but I could see that he was a little groggy. He struck at me wildly; but I stepped to one side and he missed, and as he went by I plunged my knife between his ribs. With a single, hideous shriek he sank to the floor and lay still; then I turned toward the girl, and my eyes went wide in astonishment. For a moment I could not believe their testimony.

"Dian!" I cried. "It is you?"

She ran to me and threw her arms around my neck. "David!" she sobbed. We stood there clasped in each other's arms, and it was a couple of minutes before either of us could speak.

"David," she said at last, "I couldn't believe my eyes when I recognized you shortly after you entered the room. I was quite sure that you had not recognized me, because my back was toward you; and it was all that I could do to keep from crying out to you; but I didn't because it would have distracted your attention from Moko."

"Tell me how you happen to be here," I said.

"It is a long story, David," she replied. "Wait until we have more time. Right now we should be thinking of getting out of here, and Moko has told me the way."

"Yes," I replied, "I heard; but I have a problem. There are two other prisoners here whom I should help to escape: Zor of Zoram, who was captured with me; and Kleeto, a girl from Suvi, who befriended us and made it possible for us to obtain the apparel of Jukans, which has served to at least partially disguise us."

"We must try to help them," said Dian, "and I suppose that you have some plan fully worked out."

"That is the trouble," I replied. "I have none," and then I explained the difficulties which confronted me.

When I had concluded she shook her head. "It seems almost hopeless," she said; "but I hate to abandon them."

"There is one thing that we must do, and that is get out of this room before some one comes and dis-

covers us with the body of Moko. Suppose we follow the corridor now and ascertain if it really leads
to freedom; then we will be in a better position to
make our plans for the future."

Before we left the chamber I fixed up the broken
door as best I could, lest it attract attention and indicate the avenue by which we had escaped; then I
dragged Moko's body out into the dark corridor.

"If they should find it in this room," I said, "it is
from this room that their search would start; and
naturally if they knew about the corridor, they would
immediately jump to the conclusion that we had
escaped in that way; but if it isn't here, they won't
know where to start."

"You are right," said Dian, "for no one knew that
Moko came to this room, nor would they look for
me here because this is not the room in which I was
imprisoned. Moko brought me here."

Hand in hand, Dian and I followed the dark corridor until finally we came to a heavy wooden gate
that barred further progress.

"Beyond this should lie freedom," I said, as I felt
over it for the latch.

⤳ II ⤳

THE cave which lay beyond the gate was of lime-stone formation in a hillside just outside the village. Enough light came through the outer opening to dimly illuminate the interior immediately about us. We could not immediately determine the extent of the cave; but while the walls at one side were dis-cernible, at our left they were lost in darkness out of which trickled a little stream of clear, cold water that made its way across the floor to disappear through the outer opening.

My greatest concern was that the cave might be the lair of some wild animal; but we heard nothing and there was no odor to substantiate my fears; and when we walked to the opening we realized there would be little danger on that score, for there was a sheer drop of about twenty feet to the floor of a wooded ravine. We were even safe from the more dangerous winged reptiles of Pellucidar because of the heavy growth of forest in the ravine, through which only the smaller winged creatures could fly. A tree, which grew close to the cliff at one side of the opening, would furnish us a means of descent whenever we chose to leave the cave, which would have been immediately had it not been for Zor and Kleeto.

I didn't like the idea of remaining in the cave, however, as I knew it was an avenue sometimes used by members of the royal family and therefore we might be discovered at almost any moment. Neither did I relish the idea of making a camp outside of the cave, because of our proximity to the village.

Not wishing to leave Dian alone in the cave, I took her with me and descended the tree to the ground, from which vantage point we discovered that there were many caves in the cliff. I investigated several of them and finally found one, the mouth of which could easily be barricaded. It was small and dry, and after carrying in leaves and grasses, with which we covered the floor, we had as snug and comfortable a home as any Pellucidarian might wish for. From the trees I gathered nuts and fruits while Dian dug tubers from the ground, and thus supplied with provisions we returned to our cave to rest and plan.

This was the first time that we had had a moment of leisure in comparative safety since I had found Dian again, and so I took advantage of it to have Dian tell me of the circumstances that had led up to her imprisonment in the village of Meeza.

She said that when my warriors returned to Sari, they reported that I had been killed in the battle with the warrior-women. Do-gad, nephew of the king of Suvi, had been a visitor in Sari at the time; and when he had found that I was dead he had constantly annoyed her with importunities to become his mate. Depressed by grief and disgusted with the man, she had been very short with him, commanding him to leave Sari; and when he had continued to remain there, scheming to obtain her, she had Ghak, the king of Sari, send him away. It was only because he was the nephew of the king of Suvi that he had escaped with his life.

Notwithstanding the reports that had been brought to her, Dian would not believe that I was dead, and organized an expedition to go in search of me.

The route which the expedition had to take lay through the country of the Suvians and there, much to Dian's surprise, they were received in a hostile manner by the King of Suvi, whose mind had been poisoned against the Sarians by Do-gad, his nephew.

Her camp was surrounded and attacked by a force of warriors greatly outnumbering her own.

Naturally her force was defeated and Dian was taken prisoner. Dian was taken before the king.

"I am sorry," he said, "that you are a woman. Were you a man, I would know how to treat you, for the affront you have put upon me deserves death."

"What affront?" asked Dian.

"Without reason, you ordered Do-gad, my nephew, expelled from Sari."

"Is that what he said?" she asked.

"Yes," replied the king, "and he also told me that he barely escaped with his life."

"Did he tell you why he was expelled from Sari?" demanded Dian.

"Because he was a Suvian," replied the king.

"That is not true," said Dian. "He heard that my mate was dead, and he importuned me to become his mate. I refused; but he continued to annoy me. It was then that I told him to leave Sari. Had he left at once, all would have been well; but he persisted in remaining and annoying me; then I had to ask Ghak to send him away. Ghak was furious, and so Do-gad was indeed fortunate to have escaped with his life."

"If you have spoken the truth," said the king, "it is Do-gad who will be punished, not you."

"I have spoken the truth," said Dian, "and that you should know because Do-gad's statement that he was driven from Sari because he was a Suvian is silly. The Suvians and Sarians have been on friendly terms since the establishment of the Empire of Pellucidar. Many Suvians, as you know, have come

to Sari and been treated royally. We are not so
stupid as to wantonly incur the enmity of an ally
who has always been one of the strongest supporters
of the empire."

The king nodded. "You speak with reason, and I
am sure now that you have spoken the truth. I am
sorry that my warriors attacked your camp and that
you have been subjected to the indignity of arrest.
You are free to go, or you may remain, as you wish;
but tell me, why did you come to Suvi?"

"I have never believed the rumors that David,
Emperor of Pellucidar, is dead," replied Dian. "With
my warriors, I was going to search for him."

"I will furnish warriors to take the places of those
who were killed," said the king, "and you may continue on your way."

"It is too late," replied Dian, "for the only two
men who could guide us to the place where David
was last seen were killed. I shall have to return to
Sari to obtain other guides."

"You shall have an escort then back to Sari," said
the king.

Do-gad, when he heard of what had happened

and that he was to be punished, escaped from the village with about a score of his followers. They followed the trail toward Sari for one march, and then lay in wait for Dian and her escort.

Without thought of danger, Dian's escort walked into the ambush; and when Dian saw what had happened and that Do-gad's party out-numbered hers and was almost certain to be victorious, she escaped during the fight.

As Do-gad and his men were between her and Sari, she sought to make a detour so as to avoid and elude them.

Pellucidar is a savage world in which a lone woman is most helpless. First one danger and then another drove her farther and farther away from Sari. Every time she sought to turn back, something barred her way; and then finally she became aware that Do-gad was on her trail, and her one thought then was to escape from him. How long and how far she wandered, she had no idea. That she escaped so many dangers was a miracle; but at last she fell into the hands of the Jukans, and had long since given up hope of escape when Fate drew me to her. But now that we were together again all that we had passed through seemed as nothing by comparison with the deep joy that we experienced in the renewal of the companionship that we had thought lost forever.

Dian told me the news of our friends in Sari and, best of all, that the Federated Kingdoms of Pellucidar were continuing loyal to the Empire. Once before, when I had been long absent, the Federation had started to disintegrate; but now it appeared that danger of this was past. All that concerned us now was to plan for escape with Zor and Kleeto.

Once more I set to work making weapons, this time two bows and a supply of arrows for both Dian and myself, as well as two short spears. These were weapons in the use of which Dian was proficient, and I had no doubt but that the two of us could win through to Sari once we had left the Valley of the Jukans behind. It was tragic that we must jeopardize this chance because of Zor and Kleeto, but there was nothing else that we could in honor do; and so, while I worked upon my weapons, I sought also for a reasonable plan whereby I might hope to bring Zor and Kleeto out of the village.

≍ 12 ≍

BY THE time my weapons were completed, I had formulated a plan for releasing Zor and Kleeto which I hoped would prove effective, although it entailed considerable risk. The worst part of it was that it entailed leaving Dian alone in the cave, without protection, while I entered the city. I didn't like it because of this, and she didn't like it because of the risk which I would have to run, of capture; but there seemed no other way, and so I decided to make my attempt immediately.

With a brownish pigment, which we made by crushing a certain variety of nuts, Dian lightly traced lines and wrinkles on my face, in an effort to disguise me; and when she had completed her task she said she would scarcely have known me herself, so greatly had the procedure changed my facial expression.

"I wish that it were all over and that you were back here with me again," she said. "I shall live in dread for your safety until your return."

"If, after you have slept three times," I told her, "and I have not returned, try to make your way to Sari."

"If you do not return, it will make no difference to me where I go," she said.

I kissed her goodby then; and, after barricading the entrance to the cave and concealing it with brush and grasses, I left and started for the village. The cave was well stocked with food, and I had taken in several gourds of water before leaving; so I knew she would be safe on the score of provisions and water for far longer than three sleeps, and I was certain that the cave was sufficiently well barricaded and hidden that she would be in no danger of discovery by either men or animals.

I made my way to the village gate, where I was

halted by the guard, which consisted of a dozen wild-eyed maniacs.

"Who are you?" demanded one. "And what do you want here?"

"I am a visitor from Gamba," I said. "I have come to join my friend, Zor, who is visiting Meeza, the king."

They conferred in whispers for awhile; and, finally, the one who had originally addressed me, spoke again. "How do we know you are from Gamba?" he demanded.

"Because I am a friend of Zor," I replied; "and he is from Gamba."

"That sounds reasonable," said one of them. "What is your name?"

"Innes," I replied, using my surname.

"'In-ess,'" the fellow repeated. "That is a strange name; so you must be from Gamba."

The others nodded their heads, sagely. "There is no doubt about it," said another; "he is from Gamba."

"I do not like the looks of it," said a third. "He has no spear. No man could travel safely all the way from Gamba with only a knife."

Evidently the fellow had a little more sense than his companions, for his objection was clean and to the point.

"That is right," said the original speaker. "You have no spear, and therefore you cannot be from Gamba."

"I tell you he is from Gamba," shouted another.

"Then where's his spear?" demanded the bright one, confidently.

"I lost it back on the plains, before I entered the forest," I explained. "I was hungry and would have eaten; but when I hurled my spear into an antelope, he turned and ran off with it. That, my wonderful friends, is what became of my spear. Come, let me in, or Meeza will be angry."

"Well," said the captain of the gate, "I think you're all right. I've thought so right along. You may come into the village. Where do you want to go?"

"I want to go to the palace of Meeza, the king," I replied.

"Why do you want to go there?" he demanded.

"Because that is where my friend, Zor, is."

Then the bright one had an idea. "How do you

know he's there," he demanded, "if you just came from Gamba?"

"Yes," demanded all the others, practically in chorus; "how do you know he's there?"

"I don't know he's there; but——"

"Ah-ah. He admits he doesn't know. He has come here for some bad purpose, and should be killed."

"Wait a minute!" I exclaimed. "You didn't let me finish. I said I didn't know that he was there; but I do know that he came to visit Meeza; and so, naturally, I assume that he is in Meeza's palace."

"Excellent reasoning," said the captain of the gate. "You may come in."

"Send someone to the palace with me," I said to the captain; "so that they will know that I am all right, and will let me in to see my friend, Zor."

To my annoyance, he detailed the suspicious one; and the two of us set off together through the narrow alleyways toward the palace. The scenes in the insane city were much the same as those I had witnessed at the time that I had first arrived, indescribably lunatic, grotesque or bestial, according to the mood of each actor; and in the plaza before the palace, the priests were still turning cartwheels around Ogar, the god of the Jukans.

My guide was still suspicious of me and did not hesitate to inform me of the fact. "I think you are an impostor and a liar," he said, "and I do not believe that you are from Gamba or that you have a friend named Zor."

"It is very strange," I said, "that you should think that."

"Why?" he demanded.

"Because you are, by far, the most intelligent man I have ever met, and so you should know that I am speaking the truth."

I could see that he was flattered for he preened himself and strutted a little before he made any reply; then he said, "Of course, I am intelligent; but you are very stupid. If you had not been, you would have known that I was joking all the time. Of course, I knew from the start that you were from Gamba."

"You are a very amusing fellow," I said. "You have a wonderful sense of humor. I am certain, now, that I shall have no difficulty in entering the palace and finding my friend, since I have a man of such high standing and great intelligence as you for my friend."

"You will have no trouble whatsoever," he assured me, "since I shall take you into the palace myself, and directly to the king's quarters."

Well, the fellow was as good as his word. He seemed to be well known and far more important than I had imagined, for the guard at the palace passed us immediately; and once more I entered the room where Goofo had received Zor and me. There was a new major-domo there, but he paid no attention to us. He appeared to be a victim of hypochondria, for he sat on the floor weeping copiously. One of the rules of the palace was that the major-domo question everyone who entered. We could not proceed farther without his permission.

"I can't be bothered," said the major-domo, when my guide asked this permission. "I am a very sick man, very, very sick."

"What's the matter with you?" I asked.

"Nothing," he said, "and that's the trouble. I am just sick of nothing."

"You are in a very bad state," I said.

He glanced up at me with a look of animation. "Do you really believe so?" he said.

"There's no doubt about it," I assured him.

"Where did you say you wanted to go?" he asked.

"I have come to visit my friend, Zor, who is the guest of Meeza, the king."

"Then what are you waiting for?" he demanded, angrily. "Get out of here and leave me alone;" so my guide and I passed on out of the chamber.

"Sometimes I think he is crazy," said my guide. "Most people are."

"I wonder if he could be," I replied.

As we passed near the kitchen where Kleeto had worked, we met her face-to-face in the corridor. She looked squarely at me but without the faintest indication of recognition. I wondered if my disguise was that effective or if Kleeto had just been too bright to show that she recognized me.

As we proceeded farther into the palace, my guide moved more and more slowly. Something seemed to be troubling him, and at last it came out.

"Perhaps you had better go on alone from here," he said.

"I don't know where to go," I replied. "Why can't you come with me?"

"Many strange things have been happening in the palace," he replied; "and Meeza may not be so glad to see a stranger."

"What has happened?" I asked.

"Well, for one thing, Moko, the king's son, has disappeared; so has the beautiful Sarian girl who was to be sacrificed to Ogar; then there was a prisoner named David, who disappeared. His hands were tied behind him, and he was locked up in a cell. He also was to have been sacrificed to Ogar; but when they went to the cell to get him, he had disappeared."

"How very strange!" I exclaimed. "Haven't they any idea what became of him, or of Moko, or of the girl from Sari?"

"Not the slightest," he replied; "but Bruma will find out what became of them, as soon as he finds another sacrifice for Ogar; then Ogar will tell him."

"I shouldn't think Bruma would have any difficulty finding a sacrifice," I said.

"Well, he has to have a very special one," replied

my guide. "It should be a man who is not a Jukan, or, perhaps, a Jukan from another village;" then he turned suddenly and looked at me strangely. I didn't have to ask, to know what was in his mind.

≍ 13 ≍

I HAD plenty on my mind as we approached the quarters of Meeza. I think I must have felt something like a condemned man who is hoping that a higher court will order a new trial, or the governor issue him a pardon. There was about that much hope, and that was about all there was. The looks that that fellow had given me seemed to have sealed my doom, for if the thought had occurred to him, it would certainly occur to Bruma, who was looking for a victim. He kept looking at me with that funny, wild expression in his eyes; and presently he said, "I think Ogar will be pleased with you."

"I hope so," I replied.

"Right ahead of us lie the quarters of Meeza," he said. "Perhaps we shall find Bruma there."

"Well," I said, "thank you for bringing me here. If you feel you might get in trouble for bringing a stranger to the king's quarters, you may leave me now, for I can find my way alone."

"Oh, no," he said. "I shall go all the way with you, because I am sure that you will be very welcome and that I shall be praised for bringing you."

Presently we entered a large room in which were many people. At the far end was a platform upon which Meeza was seated. The king was flanked on either side by some ten or twelve husky warriors, there to protect him against any of his subjects who might suddenly develop a homicidal mania. Although Meeza wore no crown, other than his feather headdress, I am sure that his head was not only uneasy but extremely insecure.

In the center of the room, a man was standing with his arms in a grotesque position; and his features were contorted into an expression of fiendish malevolence. My guide indicated him with a nod of his head and a wink, as he nudged me in the ribs with his elbow.

"He's crazy," he said. "He thinks he is Ogar's brother."

"And he's not?" I asked.

"Don't be a fool," snapped my guide. "He's crazy. I am Ogar's brother."

"Oh," I said. "He's very crazy, indeed."

The man certainly presented a most startling appearance, standing absolutely rigid, not a muscle moving, his eyes staring straight ahead. Presently a man ran forward and commenced to turn cartwheels around him. My guide nudged me again. "He's crazy, too," he said.

No one seemed to pay any attention either to the gentleman with delusions of grandeur or his whirling satellite. I could not help but think, as I watched these two, how close to the borderline of insanity some of the so-called great men of the outer crust must have been, for certainly many of them have appeared to be motivated by delusions of grandeur; and you doubtless will be able to think of several of your own time who loved to strike poses.

"Ah," said my guide. "There is Bruma now." Suddenly he appeared very excited. He seized me by the arm and dragged me across the floor toward a fat, greasy-looking individual with a feather headdress fully as large as that worn by Meeza but consisting of black feathers instead of white.

My guide grew more and more excited as we approached Bruma. I racked by brain for some plan of escape from my dilemma; but things looked pretty black for me, with, as far as I could see, not a single chance for escape. Trembling with excitement, the fellow dragged me into Bruma's presence.

"Here, Bruma," he cried, "is a——"

That was as far as he got. Suddenly he stiffened, his eyes rolled up and set, and he pitched forward to the floor at Bruma's feet, in the throes of an epileptic fit. As he lay there, jerking spasmodically and frothing at the mouth, Bruma looked inquiringly at me.

"What did he want?" he demanded.

"He was about to say, 'Here is a good friend of mine, who is looking for a man named Zor,'" I replied.

"And who are you?" he asked.

"I am Napoleon Bonaparte," I replied.

Bruma shook his head. "I never heard of you," he said. "Zor is over there, near the king; but I still think he would make a good sacrifice for Ogar."

"And Meeza doesn't think so?" I asked.

"No," replied Bruma, emphatically; then he leaned close to me and whispered, "Meeza is crazy."

My guide was still enjoying his fit, which was a lucky break for me, as it probably would give me time to find Zor and get out of there before he regained consciousness; so I left Bruma and walked over toward the throne.

It didn't take me long to find Zor; and, though I went and stood directly in front of him, he did not recognize me. People with whom he had been talking were standing near, and I did not dare reveal my identity in their presence.

Finally, I touched him on the arm. "Come with me a minute," I said. "There is a friend of yours over here, who wants to see you for a minute."

"What friend?" he demanded.

"The friend with whom you worked in the garden of Gluck," I replied.

"You are trying to trap me," he said. "That man is gone forever, unless he is recaptured. He certainly wouldn't be fool enough to come back here of his own volition."

"He is here," I said in a whisper. "Come with me, Zor."

He hesitated. What could I do? I knew that he was suspicious of all these people and that he might think this a ruse to get him off somewhere, out of sight for a moment, and murder him. The Jukans are that way. However, I could not reveal my identity while there were so many people within earshot of even a whisper. I glanced back at my guide. No one was paying any attention to him; but he seemed to be recovering from his seizure. I knew that I should have to do something quickly now before the fellow regained consciousness. As I raised my eyes from the prostrate form of my former guide, I saw Bruma's gaze fixed upon me, and then I saw him start toward me across the floor; then I turned back to Zor.

"You must come with me," I said; "and you must know that I am speaking the truth, for how else would I know about the garden of Gluck?"

"That is right," said Zor. "I did not think of that. Where do you want me to go?"

"Back to get Kleeto," I said in a whisper.

He looked at me very intently then, and presently his eyes widened a little.

"I am a fool," he said; "come." But I couldn't come for just then Bruma confronted us.

"Where is this Napolapart from?" he asked Zor. Zor looked puzzled. "Your friend, Napolapart," insisted Bruma.

"I never heard of anybody by that name," said Zor.

"Ah-ah, an impostor," said Bruma, glaring at me. "This man, Napolapart, said that he was a friend of yours."

"You misunderstood me, Bruma," I interrupted. "I said my name was Napoleon Bonaparte."

"Oh," said Zor. "Of course I know Napoleon Bonaparte very well. He is an old friend of mine."

"There is something very familiar about his face,"

said Bruma. "I think I must have known him, too. Where have I known you, Napolapart?"

"I have never been here before," I said.

"Where are you from then?" he demanded.

"From Gamba," I replied.

"Excellent!" exclaimed Bruma. "Just the man I am looking for as a sacrifice to Ogar."

Now here was a pretty mess, and mighty disheartening, too, with my plan right on the verge of success. What could I do? I had heard that crazy people should be humored; but how could I humor Bruma?

≍ 14 ≍

I AM NOT inclined to panics; but the siutation in which I now found myself tended to induce that state to a greater degree than any other which I can recall in my long experience in this savage world of danger.

Here I was, in a palace from which I could not find my way without a guide, surrounded by maniacs, all of whom were potential enemies; but the most terrifying feature of the situation lay in the fact that Dian would most assuredly be lost were I not able to return to her. I reproached myself for thus jeopardizing her safety for two who really had no hold upon my loyalty, other than that dictated by a sense of decency and common humanity. Right then, I would have sacrificed them both without a single qualm of conscience, could I, by such means, have returned to Dian. I realized that I had over-estimated both my luck and my cunning. The former seemed to have deserted me and the latter was about to be nullified by the still more cunning minds of madmen. Finally, I decided to try to bluff it through. I knew that Zor would be with me if it came to a fight; and I also knew that if we should try to fight our way from the palace, the reactions of the Jukans were unpredictable. I drew my knife and looked Bruma straight in the eyes.

"You are not going to sacrifice me to Ogar," I said in a loud tone of voice that attracted the attention of all around us, including Meeza, the king.

"Why?" demanded Bruma.

"Because I am a guest of Meeza," I replied, "and I demand his protection."

"Who is this man?" cried the king.

"His name is Napolapart," replied Bruma, "and he comes from Gamba. I shall sacrifice him to Ogar; so that Ogar will tell us what has become of Moko, your son."

I was facing away from Meeza at the time, because I was looking at Bruma and listening to him. Beyond the crowd I could see the doorway leading into the throne room. The backs of nearly all except those on the dais upon which Meeza sat were toward the door, and the attention of those on the dais was riveted upon Bruma and me; thus I was the only one to see a cadaverous figure stagger from the corridor and lean weakly against the frame of the doorway.

"Will Ogar tell us where Moko is, if you offer this sacrifice to him?" demanded Meeza of Bruma.

"If the sacrifice is acceptable to Ogar, he will tell us," replied the high priest. "If it is not acceptable, we shall have to try another."

I turned toward Meeza. "You do not need Ogar to tell you where Moko is," I said, "for I can tell you. Will you let Zor and me go in peace, if I tell you?"

"Yes," said the king.

I turned and pointed toward the doorway. "There is Moko," I said.

All eyes turned in the direction I had pointed to see Moko stagger forward into the room. He looked like a cadaver temporarily endowed with the power of locomotion. His body and his extremities were very thin, and his body was literally covered with blood that had dried and caked upon it from a now partially healed wound below his heart.

So I hadn't killed Moko, after all; and now, by an ironical trick of Fate, he had come back, perhaps to save me. I watched him stagger across the room to Meeza's throne, where he sank to the floor, exhausted.

"Where have you been?" demanded the king. There was nothing in his voice that denoted paternal affection or sympathy.

Weak, gasping for breath, Moko replied in a feeble whisper, "He tried to kill me. When I regained consciousness, I was in darkness for he had dragged me into the corridor of which only the king and his son have knowledge. He was gone, and with him the girl from Sari."

"Who was he?" demanded Meeza.

"I do not know," replied Moko.

"It must have been the man, David, who escaped from the cell in which he was confined," suggested Bruma.

"We shall find them," said Meeza. "Send warriors

out to search the forest for them, and search in the great cave in the Ravine of the Kings."

Immediately warriors started for the door, and Zor and I joined them. I do not believe that Bruma saw us go, as his attention was fixed upon Moko over whom he was chanting some weird jargon, doubtless something in the nature of a healing incantation.

"What shall we do?" asked Zor.

"We must find Kleeto," I replied; "and then try to leave the village with these warriors, pretending that we are going out to help search for David."

"You can't get a woman out of the village," said Zor. "Don't you remember what Kleeto told us?"

"That's right," I replied. "I had forgotten; but I have another way."

"What is it?"

"It is the corridor through which I escaped before; but the only trouble is that it leads to the large cave which they are going to search."

"What became of the girl from Sari?" he asked.

"I took her with me and hid her in another cave near the large one."

"Of course, you are going to take her with us?"

"Absolutely," I replied, "for when I found her with Moko, I made an amazing discovery."

"What was that?" asked Zor.

"That the girl from Sari was actually my mate, Dian the Beautiful."

"It was a fortunate chance, then, that caused you to be captured by the Jukans."

We found Kleeto in the kitchen of the major-domo. She was surprised and delighted to see us; but at first she could scarcely believe that it was I, so greatly had Dian's handiwork disguised me. She had not recognized me when she met my guide and me in the corridor; but she recalled having seen us pass.

We talked matters over and decided to enter the corridor and go as far as the rear entrance to the cave. There we should wait until the Jukans had completed their investigation and left. We were quite sure that they would not investigate the corridor; but if they did, we should simply have to keep ahead of them so as not to be detected, even if we had to come all the way back to the entrance.

Now, however, another obstacle presented itself. None of us knew how to reach the entrance to the corridor. Neither Zor nor Kleeto had ever been there, and I could not retrace my steps to it, even though my life and Dian's depended upon it.

"We shall have to attempt to pass out through the city, then," said Zor.

"You two go, then," said Kleeto. "I am sure that they would not permit me to pass."

"There must be some other way," said Zor.

"There is," I said. "You and I will go out of the village to search for David. When the Jukans have finished their search in the Ravine of the Kings, we can enter the cave and come back for Kleeto, for after you have found your way from the corridor to these quarters, you could easily retrace your steps, while I could not."

"It is a good plan," said Zor; "but it will not be necessary for you to come back with me and leave your mate, for all I shall have to do is guide Kleeto out of the palace; and it will not require two men for that."

"That is right," said Kleeto; "but I do not wish you to risk your lives for me. I never expected to escape, anyway; so you might as well go along and make sure of yours."

"David has already risked his life and that of his mate to come back here to rescue us," said Zor. "We shall take you with us, if it is possible to do so."

We left Kleeto and went out into the city, presently finding ourselves at the outer gate. As warriors were still passing through in search of me, we had no trouble in leaving the city.

We found the Ravine of the Kings full of searching warriors; so we joined them in order to be near Dian and learn if she were discovered.

"If she is," I said, "we shall have to fight, for I shall not permit her to be taken back into the city alive."

Mingling with the Jukans, and pretending to be hunting for myself, I made my way close to the cave where Dian was hidden. The barricade was still up, and the brush covered it. Nothing had been disturbed. Inside that cave, not ten feet from me, was the woman I loved, the only woman I had ever loved, the only woman I ever should love. She was doubtless worrying as much about my safety as I had worried about hers; and yet I dared not call out to let her know that I was there, close to her and safe, for all about us were the Jukans.

I saw some of them descending from the large cave; so I knew they had made their investigation there and that it would be safe for Zor to enter as soon as the searchers had left the ravine and make his way through the corridor to the interior of the palace.

There may not be any such thing as time in Pellucidar; but I think an eternity must have passed before the Jukans gave up their search in the ravine and left it. Zor and I had managed to conceal ourselves without appearing to do so, so that no one noticed that we remained behind when the others left.

"And now," I said to Zor, "you can make your attempt to reach Kleeto and bring her back here. The entrance to the corridor is directly opposite the mouth of the cave. After you enter the corridor, always keep your left hand against the wall; and you will be bound to retrace my steps through the palace and the corridor;—" I stopped aghast, as a recollection came suddenly to my mind.

"What's the matter?" demanded Zor, noticing my perturbation.

"How stupid of me to have forgotten!" I exclaimed.

"What are you talking about?" he demanded.

"You will not be able to pass the gate at the farther end of the corridor," I said. "It was behind that gate that I was imprisoned, and it defied my every effort to batter it down."

"Is there no other way?" he asked.

"Yes, there is; but I do not know how you can find it. There is a doorway from the corridor to the room in which I found Moko and Dian. Perhaps you will feel it, and recognize it when you come to it; but as I recall it, it seems only a part and parcel of the wooden wall that faces most of the corridor. It is, I should say, about half way between the cave and the far end of the corridor."

"If the gate is still locked, I shall find that door," Zor assured me.

"Your chances will be mighty slim, if you have to go that way," I told him, "because I am sure that that room lay in the quarters of either Moko or Meeza, for it was near there that they had Dian imprisoned. If you are discovered there, you will certainly be destroyed. Perhaps you had better give up the idea entirely, if the gate at the end of the corridor is still fastened. We shall then have done all that we humanly could to bring Kleeto out."

"If I am not back at the end of two sleeps," said Zor, "I shall never be back; and you and your mate may commence your journey to Sari."

I bade him goodby, then, with a heavy heart, and watched him climb the tree and enter the mouth of the large cave above.

⊱ 15 ⊰

AS SOON as Zor had started upon his mission, I returned to the cave where Dian was hidden; and, making sure that no one was in sight in the ravine, I started removing the brush and the barricade. As I was doing so, I called to her; but receiving no reply I presumed that she was asleep; and so I proceeded to remove the remainder of the barrier as quietly as possible so as not to disturb her, for sleep in Pellucidar is precious.

I do not know when I have been as happy as I was at that moment. My spirits were high, for now it seemed certain to me that we had an excellent chance of escaping from the Valley of the Jukans and returning to our beloved Sari.

When I had made an opening large enough to admit my body, I crawled into the cave backwards and replaced the barrier as best I could, intending to lie down beside Dian and get a little sleep myself.

How surprised she would be when she awakened to find me there beside her. I couldn't resist the temptation to reach out and touch her. The cave was small, and she could not possibly be more than an arm's length from me; but though I felt in all directions I did not find her. It was then that the terrible truth dawned upon me—Dian was gone!

To be cast from such heights of hopefulness to such a depth of despair almost unnerved me. More like a maniac than a sane man, I felt over every inch of the floor of the cave. I found some food and water. I found my weapons, too; but no Dian.

No longer was there thought of sleep; no longer thoughts of Zor or Kleeto; only Dian mattered now.

Taking a spear and the bow and arrows that I had made for myself, I pushed away the barrier and came out into the open. For a moment I stood there, undecided. Where was I to look for Dian? Something seemed to tell me, I do not know what, that she had not been taken back into the village; and I decided to go down the ravine, away from the village, which was the direction that we should have taken to leave the Valley of the Jukans on our way towards Sari. That much I knew, because I had asked Dian the direction of our country, and she had told me which way we must go to reach it.

All through the Ravine of the Kings, the ground had recently been walked over by the searching Jukans; so that any possible trace of Dian's spoor would have been obliterated; but I hoped that if I went far enough I might eventually pick it up, for, not having the homing instinct of the Pellucidarians, I had been forced to develop myself into an excellent tracker. I could follow a spoor that an ordinary man could not detect, and I banked heavily upon this ability to pick the spoor of Dian and whomever had stolen her.

I came to the end of the Jukan forest without meeting man or beast, or finding any trace of Dian.

According to Dian's directions, I turned right here and skirted the forest. She had told me that this would lead me to the far end of the valley where I should come upon a stream, and that I should follow this stream to a small inland sea into which it emptied; then I was to follow the shore of this sea to the left. Eventually, I would see a lofty mountain peak far ahead of me, which would indicate the direction of Sari. After that, I should have to depend upon my own resourcefulness to find my way, for she could not recall any other outstanding landmark, for she, born with the homing instinct, had not needed to particularly note any of them.

I had reached the lower end of the valley and the river without seeing any trace of Dian, and had just about come to the conclusion that I had been wrong in assuming that she had been brought in this direction, whereas it was equally possible that she might have been captured by the Jukans and returned to the village. Should I return to Meeza's village or should I go on? That was the question. My better judgment told me that I should turn back; but I finally decided to go on yet a little farther; but eventually I gave it up as hopeless and turned back.

The forest in the Valley of the Jukans stops rather

abruptly where it meets the plain, although a few scattered trees dot the latter. For purposes of better concealment, I travelled just inside the edge of the forest where the plain was always visible to me and trees always within easy reach as avenues of escape from the more dangerous carnivores.

From the village of Meeza to the lower end of the valley, where I had turned back, must be about twenty miles. I had been without sleep for some time and, being practically exhausted, I sought out a tree in which I could rig myself up a sleeping platform well concealed by verdure from prying eyes, and far enough above the ground to be safe from hunting beasts; and here I was soon asleep.

I do not know how long I slept; but when I awoke I found that it had rained, for the forest was dripping with water. That the rain had not awakened me was evidence of how exhausted I must have been; but now I was refreshed, and soon I was on the ground once more, ready to continue my return journey toward the village of Meeza, the king. I was refreshed, and I was also ravenously hungry, which was an approximate index as to the length of time I had slept.

As I did not care to take the time to hunt, I gathered a little fruit with the intention of eating it on the way; but almost immediately after reaching the ground, I discovered that which drove all thought of hunger from my mind, for passing directly beneath my tree were footprints of a man and woman in the rain-soaked earth—a man and a woman who had been walking hurriedly toward the lower end of the valley. Instantly I cast aside all thought of returning to the village, convinced in my own mind that these were the footprints of Dian and her abductor.

I could not tell how old the tracks were, for I could not know how long I had slept; but I knew that the rain had been comparatively recent and that the two people had passed either during or after the storm.

This lack of means for measuring time here in Pellucidar can be extremely annoying and aggravating. I might have slept for a week of earthly time, as far as I knew; and these people might be far in advance of me, or they might be but just a short distance ahead, hidden by the trees of the forest.

As the trail remained quite distinct, I could follow it rapidly. In fact, I had adopted a dog-trot which I

Armed only with stone knives, they faced the two great brutes

had learned from experience that I could maintain for great lengths of time, as only thus could I hope to overtake them, as I could see that they had been hurrying.

Near the lower end of the valley, the trail came out of the forest; and then, far ahead, I saw two figures, as yet too far away from me to recognize. Now I no longer trotted; I ran. Often I lost sight of them for a considerable time as one or the other of us dropped down into swales or hollows; but each time that they reappeared I could see that I had gained on them.

At length, after losing sight of them for a short time, I topped a rise and saw them just below me. They were standing in a clearing facing a couple of jaloks, the fierce, wild dogs of Pellucidar; and then it was that I recognized them—Zor and Kleeto. Armed only with their crude, stone knives, they were hopelessly facing the two great brutes that were slinking toward them. Their situation would have been almost hopeless had I not happened upon them in the nick of time; and even now it was none too certain that we should all three escape alive, for the jalok is an animal of great strength and terrible ferocity.

They are man-eaters of the worst type, and hunt men in preference to any other game.

As I ran down the hill toward Zor and Kleeto their backs were toward me as they stood facing the brutes; and so they did not see me, nor did they hear my sandaled feet on the soft turf. The jaloks paid no attention to me, as they have little or no fear of man, and probably looked upon me as just another victim.

As I ran, I fitted an arrow to my bow; and when I was quite sure that I was safely in range I stopped a few paces behind Zor and Kleeto and drew a bead on the larger jalok, a huge dog which stood a good six inches higher than his mate. I drew the shaft back until the tip of the arrow touched my left hand. The bow string twanged and the arrow sank deep in the chest of the dog. Simultaneously, Zor and Kleeto wheeled about and recognized me; and both jaloks charged.

With a celerity born of long continued, urgent need of self-preservation, I had fitted another arrow to my bow and driven it into the breast of the she. The shot brought her down; but the dog, growling ferociously, the arrow protruding from his breast, came leaping toward us. It was then, when he was almost upon us, that I hurled my spear, a short, heavy, javelin-like weapon.

Fortunately for us, my aim was true, and this heavier missile brought the great beast down; and a second later I put an arrow through his heart. Similarly, I dispatched the female.

Zor and Kleeto were profuse in the expression of their gratitude. They were mystified as to how it had happened that I had been behind them. They said that they had gone to the cave where Dian had been hidden, and found it empty; and immediately had come to the conclusion that she and I had started on toward Sari.

Then I told them how it had happened that I had been behind them and of my fears that Dian had been stolen; and then when I had not been able to find any trace of her spoor I had become convinced that she had been taken back into the village.

"No," said Kleeto, "I can assure you that she has not. I should have heard of it immediately, had she been brought into the major-domo's quarters. I heard the warriors talking as they returned from the search, and it was quite evident from what they said that they had found no trace of her; so I think that you may rest assured that she is not in the village of Meeza."

Well, it was, of course, something of a relief to know that; but where was she? And who had been her abductor? I recalled that Moko had wanted her to run away with him; and I questioned Kleeto as to the possibility of its having been he who had found her hiding place and taken her away.

"It is possible," she said.

"But he had been badly wounded. The last time I saw him, he was so weak he could scarcely stand."

"Oh, he has had plenty of time to recover from that," she said.

I shook my head in despair. This baffling question of elapsed time was maddening. To me, it seemed that not more than two days had elapsed since I saw Moko fall exhausted at the foot of his father's throne, yet Kleeto assured me that there had been plenty of time for his wound to heal. How was I possibly to know, then, how long it had been since Dian had been taken from the cave? If another than Moko had taken her, it might have been a great many days ago, as measured by outer earthly time. If it were Moko, it might not have been so long ago; but still, he might have had ample time to take her where I should never find her.

The fact that I could find no trace of her spoor was the most disheartening fact of all, yet I realized that she still might have passed this way but so long ago that all traces of her passage had been obliterated.

"What are you going to do?" asked Zor.

"I am going back to Sari," I replied, "and I am going to bring an army here to the Valley of the Jukans and wipe their accursed race off the face of Pellucidar. Their hereditary taint of insanity is a menace to all mankind; and you?" I asked. "Where are you going?"

"I suppose I shall never find Rana," he replied. "It seems hopeless now to prosecute the search any further. Kleeto has asked me to come back to Suvi with her," he added, in what I thought was a rather embarrassed manner.

"Then we can continue on together," I said, "for Suvi lies in the direction of Sari; and with Kleeto as a guide, my great handicap will be nullified."

"What do you mean?" she asked.

"He can't find his way home," said Zor, laughing as though it were a huge joke.

Kleeto opened her eyes in amazement. "You mean you could not find your way back to Sari alone?"

"I'm sorry," I replied; "but I couldn't."

"I never heard of such a thing," said Kleeto.

"He says he is from another world," said Zor. "At first, I did not believe him; but now that I have come to know him, I do not doubt his word."

"What other world is there?" demanded Kleeto.

"He says that Pellucidar is round like the eggs of one of the great turtles, and hollow, too. Pellucidar, he says, is on the inside, and his world is on the outside."

"Can't anyone in your world, then, find his way home, if he gets lost?" asked the girl.

"Yes," I explained; "but not in the way that you do. Some time I shall explain it to you; but right now we have other things to think about, and the most important, at the moment, is to get as far away from the Valley of the Jukans as we can."

We started on again, then, on the long trail toward Sari; and I should have been very happy and contented, had it not been for my anxiety concerning the fate of Dian. If I only knew in what direction she had been taken. Even to know who had taken her, would have been some satisfaction; but I knew neither, and I could not even guess; and prayed that time would unravel the mystery.

We had passed out of the valley and followed the river down to the shore of the inland sea, of which Dian had told me, when we passed the skeleton of a large deer from which all the flesh had been stripped by the carnivorous creatures of all sizes and descriptions which infest Pellucidar.

So often does one come across these bleaching evidences of tragedy in Pellucidar that they occasion no comment or even a single glance; but as I passed close to this one I saw an arrow lying among the bones. Naturally, I picked it up to put it in my quiver; and, as I did so, I must have exclaimed aloud in astonishment, for both Zor and Kleeto turned questioningly toward me.

"What is the matter?" asked the former.

"I made this arrow," I said. "I made it for Dian. I always mark our arrows for identification. This one bears her mark."

"Then she has been this way," said Kleeto.

"Yes, she is on the way back to Sari," I said; then I got to thinking. It was odd that it had never occurred to me before, that I had found my weapons in the cave but not Dian's. Why should her abductor have taken her weapons and not mine? I put the question to Zor and Kleeto.

"Perhaps she came alone," suggested Kleeto.

"She would never have deserted me," I said.

Zor shook his head. "I do not understand it," he said. "Very few of the men of Pellucidar know how to use this strange weapon which you make. The Jukans certainly possess none. Who else could have shot this but Dian the Beautiful, herself?"

"She must have shot it," I said.

"But if she were stolen, her captor would never permit her to carry weapons," argued Zor.

"You are right," I said.

"Then she must be alone," said Zor, "or—or she came away with someone of her own free will."

I couldn't believe that; but no matter how much I racked my brain, it was impossible for me to arrive at any explanation.

⤳ 16 ⤳

IT IS remarkable how life adapts itself to its environment, and, I may say, especially man, who is entirely hairless and unprotected from the elements and comparatively slow and weak. Here was I, a man of the Twentieth Century, with perhaps a thousand years of civilization as my background, trekking through the wildernesses of a savage world with a man and a girl of the Old Stone Age, and quite as self-reliant and as much at home as they. I, who would not have ventured upon the streets of my native city in my shirt-sleeves, was perfectly comfor-

166

table, and not at all self-conscious, in a G-string and a pair of sandals. It has often made me smile to contemplate what my strait-laced New England friends would have thought, could they have seen me; and I know that they would have considered Kleeto an abandoned wench, yet, like practically every girl I have ever known here in Pellucidar, she was fine and clean; and virtuous almost to prudery; but she did have a failing, a failing that is not uncommon to all girls on the outer crust—she talked too much. Yet her naive and usually happy prattle often distracted my mind from the sorrow which weighed it down.

Having found that I was from another world, Kleeto must know all about it; and she asked a million questions. She was a very different Kleeto from the Kleeto I had known in the palace of Meeza, the king, for then she was suppressed by the seeming hopelessness of her position and her fear of the maniacs among whom she lived; but now that she was free and safe, the natural buoyancy of her spirits reasserted itself and the real Kleeto bloomed again.

It was quite evident to me that Zor had fallen in

love with Kleeto, and there is no doubt but what the little rascal led him on—there are coquettes wherever there are women. It was impossible to tell if she were in love with him; but I think she was because she treated him so badly. Anyway, I know it was she who suggested that he go to Suvi.

"Why did you leave Suvi, Kleeto?" I once asked her.

"I ran away," she said, with a shrug. "I wanted to go to Kali; but I got lost; and so I wandered around until I was finally captured by the Jukans."

"If you were lost," said Zor, "why didn't you go back to Suvi?"

"I was afraid," replied Kleeto.

"Afraid of what?" I asked.

"There was a man there that wished to take me as his mate, but I did not want him; but he was a big strong man, and his uncle was King of Suvi. It was because of him that I ran away, and because of him that I dared not go back."

"But now you are not afraid to return?" I asked.

"I shall have you and Zor with me," she said; "and so I shall not be afraid."

"Is this man, by any chance, named Do-gad?" I asked.

"Yes," she said. "Do you know him?"

"No," I said; "but some day I am going to meet him."

It was a strange coincidence that both Dian and Kleeto had been captured by the Jukans while they were trying to escape from Do-gad. The fellow would have plenty to account for to Zor and me.

Once again it was, to me, new country that we were passing through. In fact, so enormous is the land area of Pellucidar, so sparsely peopled is it, and so little explored, that almost all of it is new country practically untouched by man. It is, however, a vast melting pot of life where animals of nearly all the geological periods of the outer crust exist contemporaneously. I have been told that there are considerable areas entirely destitute of animal life; and I know that there are others where the reptilia of the Triassic and Jurassic Ages of the outer crust reign in undisputed possession because no other creature dare enter their domain. Other areas are peopled solely by the birds and mammals that flourished on the outer crust from the Cretaceous to the Pliocene; but by far the larger part of the Pellucidar known to me from my own exploration and from heresay is inhabited by all these forms of life, with here and there an isolated community of men living mostly in caves. Only since the founding of the Empire had there been anything approaching a city built in Pellucidar, unless one might call the underground caverns of the Mahars cities, or apply the same name to the crazy conglomeration of huts occupied by the Jukans.

One city only must always be excepted from this very general statement. That is the City of Korsar, near the north polar opening, which I believe to have been originally founded by the crew of a pirate ship which, by some miracle, found its way through the polar opening from the Arctic Ocean into Pellucidar.

The civilization of these people, however, has never spread toward the South. They are, by nature, a maritime people; but having no sun, or moon, or stars to guide them, they do not dare venture out of sight of land on the great ocean that lies at their very door, the Korsar Az.

We had slept many times, and were still moving

along the shore of the sea, when we came suddenly upon a group of enormous mastodons in a little, flat-floored valley through which a river ran. There were three mastodons in the group, a bull, a cow, and a calf; and we could see by the actions of the adults that something was amiss, for they kept running back and forth, trumpeting loudly.

We were about to give them a wide berth, when I discovered the cause of their excitement. The calf had wandered into a slough near the edge of the river and had become mired down. It would have been suicide for either the cow or the bull, with their tremendous weight, to have ventured into the soft ground in an effort to save the calf.

Like most people, I am sentimental about young animals; and when I heard that poor little fellow bawling, my heart went out to him.

"Let's see if we can get him out of there," I said to Zor.

"And get killed for our pains," replied the man from Zoram.

"Old Maj is pretty intelligent," I said. "I think he would know that we were trying to help."

Zor shrugged. "Sometimes I think that you are really a Jukan," he said, laughing. "You have some of the craziest ideas."

"Oh, well," I said, "if you're afraid, of course——"

"Who said I was afraid?" demanded Zor.

That was enough. I knew that he would come with me now, if he died for it, for the men of Zoram are especially jealous of their reputation for bravery; so I started down toward the mastodons, and both Zor and Kleeto came with me. I didn't go very close to them at first but down to the edge of the marsh about a hundred yards from them where I could look over the ground and ascertain if there were any possibilities of helping the calf. At this point there was only about twenty feet of marsh between solid ground and the river, and it was covered with driftwood that had been deposited there during high water. The surface of the marsh had dried out under the hot sun, and after testing this crust I found that it would support our weight; so the only feasible plan whereby we might get the calf out was obvious. I explained it to Zor and Kleeto, and then the three of us set about gathering larger pieces of driftwood which we placed in front of the calf to form something of a corduroy road from it to the solid ground. At first, the little fellow was frightened and started plunging when we approached him; but presently he seemed to sense that we were not going to harm him, and quieted down. The bull and cow were also very much excited at first; but after awhile they stopped their trumpeting and stood watching us. I think they realized what we were trying to do. The last few feet of our improvised road had to be laid down within a few feet of them, and was in easy reach of their trunks; but they did not offer to molest us.

With the road completed came the job of trying to get the calf onto it. He probably weighed at least a ton; so lifting him was out of the question.

Zor and I found a large log and laid it parallel and close to him; then we got a long piece of driftwood that was staunch and strong—the bole of a small tree—placed one end across the log, and slowly worked it under one of his forelegs. In the meantime, Kleeto, following my instructions, was ready with the largest piece of driftwood she could lift.

Zor and I got on the outer end of our lever and threw all our weight onto it. Time and again we repeated this, until finally the leg commenced to pull out of the muck; and, as soon as it was free, Kleeto shoved the piece of driftwood beneath it.

The calf then tried to scramble out on the roadway; but he couldn't quite make it, and so we went around to the other side and repeated the operation on his other foreleg. This was easier because he could help himself a little now with his free leg; and as soon as he had both of them on solid footing he wallowed around for a moment and finally dragged himself out.

I had never seen anything so touching as the solicitude of the bull and cow when the little fellow finally stood beside them on solid ground. They felt him all over for a moment or two to see that he was all right and then dragged him away from the edge of the marsh.

Kleeto, Zor, and I sat down on the big log to rest, for it had been fatiguing work. We expected the mammoths to go away; but they didn't. They stopped a couple of hundred feet from us and watched us.

After we had rested, we started on again, looking for a place to cross the river; and as soon as we did the bull started toward us, followed by the cow and the calf. That didn't look so good, and we kept close to the edge of the marsh so that we could escape them if they showed any disposition to be nasty. We kept glancing back over our shoulders, and presently I noticed that the mastodons were not gaining on us. Apparently it was merely a coincidence that they were going in the same direction that we were.

We had to go quite a little distance up river before we found a place where we could make a safe crossing. It was not a very large river, and the bottom where we crossed was gravelly. When we reached the opposite bank we saw that the mastodons were entering the river behind us.

Well, they tagged along after us until we found a safe place to camp. They didn't approach very close to us at any time; and when we stopped they stopped.

"It looks as though they were just following us," said Kleeto.

"It certainly does," agreed Zor; "but I wonder why?"

"You've got me," I said. "I don't think they intend to harm us. They don't show any signs of nervousness or excitement, such as they would if they were angry or afraid of us."

"Old Maj isn't afraid of anything," said Zor. Maj is the Pellucidarian name for the mastodon.

"I'm going to see if they're friendly," I said.

"You better locate a nice tree before you try anything," said Zor; "and be sure it's a big one. That old bull could uproot almost anything around here."

We had halted near some caves, where we intended to camp, and I figured that if the mastodons were inclined to be unfriendly I could beat them to the cave we had selected before they could overhaul me; at least I hoped so.

I walked slowly toward them, and they just stood there looking at me without showing any signs of nervousness. When I was about a hundred feet from them, the calf started to come toward me; then the cow moved a little restlessly and made a funny little noise. I guess she was trying to call him back, but he came on; and I stood still and waited. He stopped two or three times and looked back at the cow and the bull; but each time he came on again and, finally, he stopped a few feet from me. He stuck his trunk way out in front of him, and I reached out my hand very slowly and touched it. I scratched it a little bit; and he came a step or two closer. I put my hand on his head then and scratched his forehead. He seemed to like it; but presently he started winding his trunk around me, and I did not like that; so I took it and unwound it forcibly.

The bull and the cow hadn't moved; but, believe me, they were watching us. All of a sudden the cow raised her trunk and trumpeted; and the little fellow wheeled around and went lumbering back to her as fast as he could go, while I walked back and joined Zor and Kleeto.

That was the beginning of a very strange friendship, for when we awoke after our sleep the mastodons were still hanging around; and they tagged along behind us for every march after that for a long time.

I used to talk to them a lot and call them Maj; and once when they were not near camp when we awoke after a sleep I shouted the name several times; and presently the three of them came out of the nearby forest, where they had evidently been feeding. We had become quite accustomed to them, and they to us, with the result that they often came quite close to us. In fact, I often stroked their trunks, which, for some reason, they seemed to enjoy; but why they were following us we could not guess, nor did we ever know. The closest conjecture that I could arrive at was that they were grateful to us for having saved the calf from the marsh in which he would surely have died had we not come along. Their presence with us more than repaid us for our efforts in behalf of the calf, for while they were with us we were never once menaced by any of the many predatory animals which abound in the country through which we passed, as even the most savage of them respect the strength of Maj.

We had slept many times since leaving the Valley of the Jukans; so that I knew that we had travelled a considerable distance, when we prepared to make camp after a long march at the foot of a cliff in which there was a cave where we might find security while we slept. The remains of a campfire in front of the cave indicated that it had been used comparatively recently; and the face of the cliff beside the mouth of the cave bore evidence that a number of wayfarers had found shelter there in times past, for many of them had scratched their marks in the limestone, a custom which is quite prevalent among the more intelligent tribes of Pellucidar, where each individual has his own personal mark which answers the purpose of a signature.

As I glanced at them casually, my attention was suddenly riveted upon one evidently made quite recently. It was an equilateral triangle with a dot in the center. It was Dian's mark. I called the attention of Kleeto and Zor to it; and they became quite as excited as I.

"She has been here quite recently and alone," said Zor.

"What makes you think she was alone?" I demanded.

"If there had been another with her, he also would have made his mark," replied Zor; "but hers is the only one freshly made."

Could it have been that Dian had deliberately deserted me? I could not believe it, and yet I knew that the evidence must seem conclusive to anyone who did not know Dian the Beautiful as well as I.

⚡ 17 ⚡

IT WAS at this camp that the mastodons left us. When we awoke I called them many times; but they did not come; and I think we all felt a little depressed about it as we started off once more on the long trek toward Sari.

For some inexplicable reason, I was haunted by a presentiment of evil after the mastodons left us; nor was I alone in this. Both Zor and Kleeto shared my depression. As though to further accentuate our mood, the sky became overcast with dark and ominous clouds; and presently there broke upon us a terrific electrical storm. The wind howled about us, almost hurling us to the ground. The air was filled with flying leaves and branches; and the trees of the forest swayed and groaned ominously. Our situation was most precarious, with trees crashing down all about us. The rain fell in great masses which swept against us with staggering force. I had never seen such a storm before in Pellucidar.

Constantly buffeted by wind and water, we staggered on until at last we came to a comparatively open space which we felt would be far safer than the denser forest. Here we huddled together with our backs toward the storm, waiting like dumb creatures for the battle of the elements to subside.

Great animals, which ordinarily would have threatened our very existence, passed close by us as they fled before the storm; but we had no fear of them for we knew that they were even more terrified than we, and that hunting and feeding were far from their thoughts. Aside from the danger from flying branches, we felt comparatively safe; and so were not as alert as customarily, although, as a matter of course, we could have heard or seen little above the storm and the blinding rain. The crashing thunder, following peal after peal, almost continuously, combined with the howling wind to drown out any other sound.

At the very height of the storm we were suddenly seized from behind by powerful fingers. Our weapons were wrenched from us and our hands secured behind our backs; then, at last, we saw our captors. There were fifteen or twenty of them, the largest men I have ever seen. Even the smallest of them stood fully seven feet in height. Their faces were extremely ugly, and a pair of great, tusk-like yellow teeth imparted no additional beauty to them. They appeared to be very low in the scale of human evolution, being entirely naked and armed only with the most primitive weapons—a very crude stone knife and a club. In addition to these, each of them carried a grass rope.

They paid no more attention to the storm than as though it did not exist; but they seemed mightily pleased over their capture.

"Good," grunted one, pinching Kleeto's flesh.

"What do you intend doing with us?" I demanded.

One of them leaned close to me, leering and blowing his foul breath in my face. "Eat you," he said.

"Stay out of Azar, if you do not want to be eaten," said another.

"Azar!" ejaculated Kleeto. "Oh, now I know. All my life I have heard of the man-eating giants of Azar. There is no hope for us now, David."

I must admit that the outlook was not very bright; but it has been my custom never to abandon hope. I tried to cheer Kleeto up a bit, and so did Zor; but we were not very successful, not even when the storm passed as quickly as it had broken upon us and the sun shone down again out of a clear sky, suggesting, as I told her, that our storm might clear and our good luck return as had the sun.

The Azarians dragged us along through the forest; and presently we came to a palisaded village, or rather, I should say, a palisaded enclosure, for after we entered it we found there no sign of habitation whatsoever. The storm had wreaked quite a little havoc in the enclosure, several trees having been blown down, one of them having levelled a portion of the palisade.

There were a number of Azarian women and chil-

dren in the enclosure, all quite as uncouth and repulsive as the males, while tied to individual trees
were several human beings like ourselves, evidently
prisoners.

Our captors tied us to trees and then set about re-
building the damaged palisade. The women and
children paid very little attention to us. A few of the
former came up and pinched our flesh to see what
condition we were in, an all too suggestive gesture.

I was tied to a tree close to one of the prisoners
who had been there before us, and I got into conversation with him. "How long will it be," I asked him,
"before they eat us?"

He shrugged. "When our flesh is in a condition
that suits them," he replied. "They feed us princi-
pally on nuts with a little fruit, and never give us
any flesh."

"Do they abuse you?" I asked.

"No," he replied, "for that would retard our fattening. They may sleep many times before they eat
any of us, for they consider human flesh a rare deli-
cacy, which they do not often enjoy. I have been
here for more sleeps than I can remember; and I

have seen only two prisoners eaten. That is not a pleasant sight. They break all their bones with clubs, and then roast them alive."

"Is there no chance to escape?" I asked.

"Not for us," he said. "Two escaped during the storm. Their trees blew down, breaking their ropes, and they ran off into the forest with their hands still bound behind them. They will not last very long; but their deaths will be easier thus than as though they had remained here to be beaten and roasted. I feel very sorry for one of them. She was a beautiful girl from Sari—Dian the Beautiful, the man called her."

For a moment I was speechless. The shock was as great as a physical blow. Dian out in that savage forest with her hands bound behind her! I must do something; but what could I do? I started rubbing the rope that bound my wrists against the rough bark of the tree behind me. It was something, no matter how hopeless. Perhaps the man who escaped with her would find a way to free her, I thought. That gave me a little hope.

"You say a man escaped with her?" I asked.

"Yes."

"Who was he? Do you know?"

"He was a man from Suvi. His name was Do-gad."

That was another terrific jolt. Of all the men in the world, that it should have been Do-gad. Now, more than ever, I must escape.

The Azarian warriors finished the palisade and lay down to sleep. They, and their women and their children slept on the ground like beasts, their only shelter the shade of the trees beneath which they lay.

When they awoke, the men went out to hunt. They brought back animals, for they always craved flesh. The women and children gathered fruit and nuts, quantities of which were fed to us to fatten us.

Sleep after sleep came and went; and constantly, when I was unobserved, I rubbed my bonds against the rough bark of the tree. I knew that I was making progress; but after I gained my freedom what might I do with it? There were always Azarians inside the palisade; the palisade was too tall for me to scale; and there was but a single gate, which remained closed always; but still there was always the chance that some combination of circumstances might open the way for me. My greatest handicap, however, lay in the fact that I should have to release Zor and Kleeto, for I could not desert them. They, too, were working to cut their bonds; but it was more than could possibly be expected that we should all achieve the desired results simultaneously.

And so time dragged its slow way even in this timeless world; and my thoughts were constantly upon Dian out there somewhere alone, always in tragic danger if not already dead. But was she alone? Yes, even though Do-gad had escaped with her, I was positive that she was alone, if she were still alive, for she would have found some way to escape from him or she would have killed herself.

Such were my unhappy thoughts as, tethered to a tree, I waited there in the compound of the man-eating giants of Azar for a horrible fate that now seemed inevitable.

≳ 18 ≳

THE long, Pellucidarian day dragged on. It was the same day upon which I had broken through the earth's crust from the outer world thirty-six years before, and it was exactly the same time of day—high noon—for the stationary sun still stood at zenith. It was the same day and hour that this world was born, the same day and hour that would see its death —the eternal day, the eternal hour, the eternal minute of Pellucidar.

With the exception of two or three women and some half-grown children, the Azarians slept. Those who remained awake were busy around the pit in the

center of the compound. It was a pit about seven
feet long, two feet wide, and some foot and a half
or two feet deep. They were removing ashes from
it. They worked in a very slovenly manner, scoop-
ing the ashes out with their hands and throwing
them upon the ground. The children, vicious little
beasts, quarrelled among themselves. Sometimes a
woman would cuff one of them, sending it sprawling.
I had never seen any sign of affection among these
people, who were much lower than the beasts.

When they had removed all the ashes they made
a bed of dry leaves and twigs in the bottom of the
pit. Over these they placed larger branches, and
finally over all they placed several good-sized logs.
Knowing what I did about them, it was all too suggestive. They were preparing for the feast. Who
would be the first victim?

A kind of terror that was almost panic gripped me.
The horror of such a death was borne in more forcibly upon me now that I actually saw the preparations in progress. Every moment that no eye was
turned upon me, I worked frantically to sever my
bonds. It was an arduous and fatiguing labor, made

more arduous and fatiguing by the conviction that it was futile. I saw that Zor and Kleeto were also working upon their bonds; but with what success I had no way of knowing.

The Azarians had taken my bow-and-arrows and spear away from me at the time we were captured, and had left them lying there upon the ground; but they had neglected to take our knives. I presume that they felt that with our hands bound behind us we could not use our weapons. Perhaps the best reason that they had not taken them, however, was the fact that they are very stupid and unimaginative. Yet, perhaps their indifference was warranted, for what could I accomplish single-handed against these huge creatures?

As these thoughts were passing through my mind, I continued to work upon my bonds and suddenly I felt the last strand part. My hands were free! I still thrill to the memory of that moment; but though my freedom availed me nothing it still imparted to me a new sense of self-confidence. Had I not felt the responsibility of my loyalty to Zor and Kleeto, I should have made a run for it, for I was confident that

I could scale the palisade at a point where it was topped by a small tree which the Azarians had leaned against it at an angle of about forty-five degrees; but because of Zor and Kleeto I had to abandon the idea.

Presently the Azarians who had been sleeping began to awaken. Some of the males came and inspected the preparations that the women and children had been making; then one, who appeared to be the chief, came over to us. He examined us carefully, feeling of our ribs and pinching our thighs. He stopped longest before Kleeto; then he turned to two of the warriors who had accompanied him. "This one," he said.

The two warriors removed her bonds. From where I stood I could see that she had almost succeeded in wearing them away; but the Azarians did not seem to notice. So Kleeto was to be the next victim! What could I do to prevent it, I with my puny, little stone knife against all those Gargantuan giants? But I determined to do something. I planned it all out carefully. When the attention of the Azarians was distracted from us, I would rush over and cut Zor's bonds with my knife; then the two of us would throw ourselves upon them, hoping to disconcert them momentarily while at least one of us three escaped over the top of the palisade.

They dragged Kleeto over beside the pit, and here ensued a discussion which I could not overhear; and then something happened which gave me an inspiration. From beyond the palisade I heard the trumpeting of a mastodon. We had seen no signs of the great beasts in this locality other than the three which had followed us. Could that be Old Maj himself out there looking for us? It seemed incredible; and yet there was a chance; and, like a drowning man grasping for a straw, I grasped at that absurdity, and raising my voice I called to the great beast as I had in the past. Instantly every eye was focussed upon me; but I called again, and this time louder, and, from the near distance, came a trumpeting reply; but the Azarians did not seem to connect the two, and turned once more to their preparations for their grisly feast. They threw Kleeto to the ground, and while some held her there, others went to fetch clubs with which to break her body; and then I raised my voice again and shouted loudly for Maj; then while every Azarian eye was intent upon Kleeto, I ran quickly to Zor and cut the remaining strands of his bonds.

"They come," he whispered. "Listen!"

"Yes." I could plainly hear the crashing of great bodies through the trees. The trumpeting rose to such proportions that the Azarians momentarily turned their attention from Kleeto and looked questioningly in the direction from which the disturbance came. Then, of a sudden, the palisade flew apart like matchwood, and the great bulk of Maj burst into the village.

The astounded Azarians stood in helpless astonishment. Zor and I rushed to Kleeto's side and snatched her to her feet; and then Maj and his mate and the calf were upon us.

"Maj, Maj," I cried, hoping that he would recognize us; and I am sure that he did. Some of the Azarians sought to protect their village with their clubs and knives, and these the mastodons lifted with their trunks and threw high into the air; then Old Maj seized me and I thought that he was going to kill me, but instead he charged on through the village and holding me low beneath his tusks he lowered his head and crashed through the palisade on the opposite side of the village from that which he had entered.

He lumbered on with me for a long time, stopping at last close to a river which ran through a broad plain; then he set me down.

I had been saved; but where were Zor and Kleeto? Had they been as fortunate as I, or were they still prisoners of the man-eating giants of Azar?

I was pretty well shaken by that arduous trip through the forest, for I may say that with all his good intentions Old Maj had handled me rather roughly; so the moment he released me I lay down in the long grass beside the river to rest, and Old Maj stood guard above me, weaving his great bulk to and fro, his little red-rimmed eyes gazing back along the trail we had come. Presently he raised his trunk and trumpeted shrilly, and immediately he was answered from the distance. I recognized the higher note of the cow and the squeal of the calf, and wondered if Zor and Kleeto were with them.

Presently the two mastodons came into view; but

they were alone. What had been the fate of my companions? Had they escaped, or were they still captives in the village of the Azarians? I was depressed not only because of my apprehension as to them, but as to my own situation as well. Had there been the slightest likelihood that I could have succored them I should have been glad to return to the village and make the attempt; but it was quite unlikely that I could find my way back, and even had I been able to do so there was practically no chance that I might have been able to aid them.

Their loss meant a great deal to me, for more than sentimental reasons even, for I had been depending upon Kleeto to lead me back to the vicinity of Sari. Now, without a guide, and with no course to follow, the chances were very remote that I should ever reach my home again. Still further weighing down my spirits was my concern over the fate of Dian. I had escaped from the Azarians; but I was far from happy, and perhaps some worse fate lay before me in the endless and aimless wandering that lay ahead.

⪦ 19 ⪧

IMAGINE yourself the size of a microscopic mi-
crobe and that you are standing on the outside of a
tennis ball, somehow miraculously suspended in
space. The surface of the tennis ball would drop
away from you in all directions, and no matter where
you looked there would be a well defined horizon.
Suddenly you are transported to the interior of the
tennis ball, which is illuminated by a stationary sun
hanging in its exact center. In all directions the interior surface of the ball would curve upward and
there would be no horizon. Thus it was with me, as
I stood beside that river in Pellucidar. It was as
though I stood in the center of a shallow bowl some

three hundred miles in diameter. The air was clear, the sun was bright, and under these conditions I assumed that the limit of my vision was about one hundred and fifty miles, although of course no object was clearly discernible at such extreme distance —the periphery of my bowl merely faded off into a vignette, blending into the haze of the distance which was beyond the range of my vision.

At a hundred miles, a single tree standing upon a plain was discernible, whereas a mountain was not. That was because, beneath the eternal noon-day sun, the tree cast a shadow, while the mountain did not, and there being no sky to form a sharply contrasting background it simply merged with the landscape behind it and appeared as level ground.

I may say that in order to recognize a tree at a hundred miles I was largely aided by my imagination; but I could easily distinguish land from water, even at the periphery of my bowl, for the water reflected the sunlight more strongly. I could see the river, upon the bank of which I stood, emptying into an ocean some fifty miles away.

To me, these aspects of the Pellucidarian scene

were now familiar; but you may well imagine how strangely they must have affected Perry and me when we first broke through the crust from the outer world. However, though familiar with it, I have never become entirely reconciled to the loss of a horizon. Always, for some reason, it imparts to me a sense of frustration, perhaps because of a subconscious feeling that I should be seeing farther than I do. Again, notwithstanding the enormous size of my bowl, I have a quite definite feeling that I am a victim of claustrophobia. I am in a bowl from which I can never climb, because no matter how far I travel or in what direction the rim of the bowl moves steadily forward at the same rate. Fortunately for my peace of mind and my sanity, I do not let my thoughts dwell long upon this subject; and I only mention these things here to give you of the outer crust a little clearer conception of some of the conditions which pertain in Pellucidar so that you may better visualize the weird scene which is now commonplace to me.

As I stood there in the center of that great bowl, my only companion the great mastodons, I sought to arrive at some logical plan for the future.

It was within the range of possibility that the body of water which I saw in the distance was that great ocean, uncharted and unexplored, which has as many names as there are tribes along its shores. I had known it in one place as the Lural Az, in another as the Darel Az, and, below the Land of Awful Shadow, the Sojar Az.

If my assumptions were correct, I might follow its shoreline to Amoz and thence to Sari.

I could see islands far out upon its bosom, isles of mystery whose secrets I could never know. What strange men and beasts inhabited those emerald gems floating upon the azure sea? The inaccessible and the unknowable always intrigue my imagination; and once more I determined, as I had often before, that if I were fortunate enough to return to Sari, I would build a seaworthy vessel and explore the waters of Pellucidar.

How little I knew of this land in which I had spent so many years! When I first came here, I spoke authoritatively upon many subjects concerning which I realize now I had little or no knowledge. I assumed, for instance, that those things which came within

the range of my experience were typical of all Pellucidar. I assumed, for instance, that the Mahars,
those ramphorynchus-like reptiles who were the dominant race of that portion of the inner world with
which I was familiar, were dominant throughout the
entire area of Pellucidar; but now I realize that I
do not know this, for the land area of Pellucidar is
enormous, and I had seen only a very tiny portion
of it.

Likewise my assertion that three-quarters of the
surface of Pellucidar is land, giving a total land area
considerably greater than that of the outer crust, was
based solely upon Perry's theory that depressions
upon the outer crust were protuberances upon the
inner crust; so that land areas in Pellucidar corre-
sponded roughly with the oceans of the outer world;
but of course that is only a theory, and I do not know
that it is true.

With a seaworthy ship and the navigating instru-
ments that Perry has been able to fabricate, I could
become a Columbus, a Magellan, a Captain Cook,
and a Balboa, all rolled into one. For an adventur-
ous spirit, the prospect was most alluring; but inas-

much as right at the moment I didn't even know my way home the realization of it seemed slightly remote, to say the least.

I followed the river down toward the sea until I found a cave where I might sleep; and after gathering some berries and digging a few tubers with which to partially satisfy my hunger, I crawled in and fell asleep.

As I have repeated, probably *ad nauseam*, I do not know how long I slept; but when I emerged from my cave the mastodons were nowhere in sight, and though I called them many times they did not appear; and I never saw them again.

Now I was indeed alone, and I had never felt so lonely in my life. The company of the great beasts had not only given me a feeling of security but of companionship, and now I felt as one might feel who had lost his last friend in all the world. With a sigh, I turned my face toward the great sea; and, armed only with a puny stone knife, set out once more upon my perilous and almost hopeless quest for Sari.

Before long I found material for weapons; and once more I set to work to fabricate a bow, some

Once more I set to work to fabricate a bow

arrows, and a spear. I kept at this steadily until the job was completed. Of course, I don't know how long it took; but I was quite ready to sleep again by the time my weapons were completed. You have no idea with how much greater sense of security I faced the future, now that I was again adequately armed.

As I approached the river I saw a number of low hillocks in the distance. They appeared to be devoid of vegetation, which is rather unusual in this world of lush tropical verdure; but what aroused my interest more than this was the fact that I saw a number of animals moving about upon them. They were too far away for me to identify them; but because of their numbers I assumed that they were a herd of herbivorous animals. As I had eaten no meat for some time, I welcomed the opportunity to make a kill and therefore set about approaching as close as I could to them without being seen. I found good cover in the gorge of the river from which I could not even see the hillocks; so I knew that the animals would not be able to apprehend me until I was quite close to them.

I advanced cautiously and as noiselessly as possible, until I felt that I was about opposite the hillocks; then I clambered up the steep river bank and wormed my way on my belly through long grass toward a point where I hoped to get a closer view of my quarry. The grass ended abruptly at the base of one of the hillocks, and as I emerged from it I came upon a scene that quite took my breath away.

The hillocks consisted of sticks and stones and boulders of all sizes; and scurrying over them were enormous ants carrying on on a Brobdingnagian scale the same activities that I had watched their diminutive cousins of the outer crust engaged in upon countless occasions. The creatures were of enormous proportions, their bodies being fully six feet long, the highest point of their heads being at least three feet above the ground—and such heads they were! These enormous heads presented a most ferocious appearance with their huge eyes, their jointed antennae, and powerful mandibles.

If you have watched the common ant in the garden carrying enormous loads often many times larger than themselves, you may be able to gain some slight

conception of the enormous strength of these creatures. Many of them carried great boulders that it
would have taken several men to lift; and I saw one
with the trunk of a good-sized tree in its mandibles.

I could now see that what I had thought were
natural hillocks were in reality enormous ant hills.
At the foot of the hills was a clearing covering many
acres where numerous ants were engaged in what,
despite my incredulity, I presently discovered were
agricultural pursuits. They labored in symmetrically
planted fields where plants and flowers were growing.
The rows were straight, and the plants equally
spaced. Not a weed was visible, and there were rows
evidently recently set out in which each plant was
covered by a large leaf to protect it from the hot rays
of the sun.

So astounded and fascinated was I that I remained
for some time watching the creatures carrying on
their building operations and caring for their crops.
Some of the workers in the field were collecting tender shoots from the growing plants and others extracting honey from the flowers and carrying their

burdens back into the ant hills. There were streams of ants moving constantly in opposite directions to and from the hills. All was activity and bustle.

I noticed that some of the ants were larger than others, and that the larger ones did no work; and then I noticed that their mandibles were much more powerful than those of their fellows, and I realized that they were the soldier ants guarding the workers.

It was all very interesting; but I realized that I could not lie there on my belly in the grass forever, watching these *Formicidian* activities no matter how enthralling they might be. I could never fill my belly with meat by watching ants at work; and so, with a sigh of regret, I arose to leave. That was an almost fatal error.

Lying quietly and almost entirely concealed by the tall grasses, the ants had not perceived me; but when I arose they were instantly conscious of my presence. I do not know whether they saw me or not, for notwithstanding their large eyes it is possible that they may be blind, as some species of ants are; but ants do not need to see, since they are furnished with delicate organs of hearing in the head, in the three thoracic and two of the abdominal segments, and in the shins of the legs, in addition to which their elbowed feelers or antennae are abundantly supplied with tooth-like projections connected with nerve endings which function as olfactory organs; therefore, though they might not be able to see me, they could certainly hear me or smell me—at any rate, they knew I was there; and several of the great soldier ants started toward me.

One look at those terrible faces and formidable mandibles was enough. I turned to beat a retreat; but glancing back over my shoulder I saw that I was too late. The soldier ants were racing after me on their six powerful legs much faster than I could run. My back was to the wall! It was a case of fight or die or, perhaps, fight *and* die.

I wheeled, and as I wheeled I fitted an arrow to my bow. My first shaft drove straight through one of the great eyes of the leading ant, and it dropped, writhing, to the ground. I brought down another an instant later, and then two more in quick succession; but my stand was futile. The others were upon me, and I was borne to the ground.

I remember the thoughts that flashed through my mind—that death had overtaken me at last, and that I was to die alone, and that no man would ever know how or where. My beautiful Dian, if she still lived, good old Perry, and my countless other friends of the inner world would never know.

I waited for a pair of those great mandibles to crush the life from me. Two of the creatures were feeling me over with their antennae, and then presently one of them picked me up by the small of my back, the pressure of the mandibles no greater than was necessary to hold me. The creature carried me as easily as you would carry a kitten, and it bore me off in that erratic manner which ants sometimes display, zig-zagging to and fro, often bumping my head or scraping my feet against obstacles or other ants.

Only occasionally did any of the other creatures pay any attention to me, though once or twice my captor stopped while another ant felt me over with his antennae. These, I thought, might be officers of the army or high officials. Perhaps they were inspecting me to see what I was and giving instructions for my disposal.

Eventually, after wandering around aimlessly, my captor headed toward a hole near the base of an ant hill. It was not a large opening, and he had difficulty in negotiating it with me in his mandibles. Twice I got stuck crossways, which was not very pleasant as the opening was rimmed with rocks. The creature tried to push me through, but he couldn't make it; so finally he laid me down, grabbed me by my legs and backed into the hole, dragging me in after him.

I realized then how the flies and caterpillars felt which I had seen dragged into the nests of ants. Perhaps, as I did, they took one last, despairing look at the beautiful world that they were leaving forever.

≍ 20 ≍

CAPTIVITY is a state sufficiently harrowing; but captivity that can end only in death in infinitely worse; and when your captors are creatures with whom you cannot communicate, the horror of the situation is increased manyfold. If I could have talked with these creatures, I might have ascertained what they intended doing with me. I might even have been able to bargain for my release; but as it was, I could do nothing but wait for the end. What that would be I could only surmise, but I assumed that I had been brought in as food.

The creature dragged me a short way into the

interior of the hill and then up a short ascending tunnel into a large chamber, which was evidently situated just beneath the surface of the ground, for there was an opening in the dome-like ceiling through which the sunlight poured.

My first hasty survey of the chamber revealed the fact that there were a number of ants in it, three of them with enormously distended abdomens hanging from the ceiling by their feet. Occasionally an ant would come through the opening in the ceiling and apparently force something down the throat of one of these creatures, which I later learned were living reservoirs of honey which supplied food for their fellows and creatures which were being fattened for food. I recalled that, as a boy, I had read of the existence of these honey-pots in some families of the *Formicidae*. I recalled that the idea had intrigued me; but I had always pictured ants as being tiny creatures; but now the sight of these enormously distended, pendant bodies was peculiarly revolting.

My captor had dropped me unceremoniously upon the floor of the chamber; then he had gone to a couple of other ants, and they had felt each over with their antennae, which I came to discover was the means they adopt for communicating with one another. After this the creature left the chamber and the other ants apparently paid no attention to me.

Naturally, uppermost in my mind were thoughts of escape; and, seeing the ants engaged in their own affairs, I moved cautiously toward the aperture through which I had been dragged into the chamber.

My hopes rose high, for I knew that I could find my way out of the ant hill, and there was a chance that I might thus escape if I moved slowly and with extreme caution so as not to attract the attention of the creatures working upon the outside of the hill; but no sooner had I reached the opening than one of the ants was upon me and, seizing me in its mandibles, it dragged me back into the room.

"Don't waste your energy," said a voice from the shadows close to the wall. "You cannot escape."

I looked in the direction from which the voice had come, and saw a figure huddled against the wall not far from me.

"Who are you?" I demanded.

"A prisoner like yourself," replied the voice.

I moved closer to the figure, for that human voice had imparted to me renewed courage and renewed hope. Even though the owner of the voice were a stranger and doubtless an enemy, he promised companionship of a sort; and among these silent, ferocious insects, companionship with another of my own species was a priceless boon.

The ants paid no attention to me as I moved closer to my fellow prisoner, for I was not going nearer to the doorway; and I finally was close enough to see him. No wonder I had not seen him before, for in the shadowed part of the chamber close to the wall he appeared as black as night. Later I was to discover that there was a slight copper tint to his skin.

"You are the only other prisoner?" I asked.

"Yes," he said. "They have devoured the others. It will probably be my turn next, though it may be yours."

"Is there no escape?" I demanded.

"None. You should know. You have just tried it and failed."

"My name is David," I said. "I am from Sari."

"I am U-Val," he said. "I come from Ruva."

"Let us be friends," I said.

"Why not?" he asked. "We are surrounded by enemies, and we shall soon be dead."

As we talked, I had been watching an ant extracting honey from one of the honey-pots depending from the ceiling. I watched it clamber down the wall and cross the floor in our direction; and then, suddenly, to my surprise, it leaped upon me and threw me to the ground upon my back and, holding me down, squirted honey into my mouth. It forced me to swallow it, too. When this forced feeding was over, the creature left me.

U-Val laughed, as I spluttered and coughed. "You will get used to it," he said. "They are fattening you for food, and they won't leave it to you to choose the kind or quantity of food which you consume. They know exactly what you should have, in what quantities, and at what intervals to get the best results. They will feed you grain presently, which they have partially digested and regurgitated. It is very good and quite fattening. You will enjoy it."

"I shall vomit," I said, disgustedly.

He shrugged. "Yes, perhaps at first; but after awhile you will become used to it."

"If I don't eat, I sha'n't get fat; and then perhaps they won't kill me," I suggested.

"Don't be too sure of that," he said. "I think we are being fattened for the queen and her young, or perhaps for the warrior ants. If we don't get fat, we shall probably be fed to the slaves and workers."

"Do you think there is any advantage in being eaten by a queen?" I asked.

"It makes no difference to me," he said.

"Possibly one might have a feeling of greater importance."

"You are joking?" he asked.

"Naturally."

"We do not joke much in Ruva," he said, "and certainly I do not feel much like joking here. I am going to die; and I do not wish to die."

"Where is Ruva?" I asked.

"You have never heard of Ruva?" he demanded.

"No," I admitted.

"That is very strange," he said. "It is a most important island—one of The Floating Islands."

"And where are they?" I demanded.

"Now where would an island float?" he demanded. "In the sea, of course."

"But what sea, and where?" I insisted.

"The Bandar Az," he explained. "What other sea is there?"

"Well, I have seen the Korsar Az," I replied, "the Sojar Az, the Darel Az, and the Lural Az. There may be others, too, that I have not heard of or seen."

"There is only one sea," said U-Val, "and that is the Bandar Az. I have heard that far away there are some people who call it the Lural Az; but that is not its name."

"If you live on an island, how do you happen to be a prisoner here on the mainland?" I asked.

"Well, sometimes Ruva floats near the mainland; and when it does we often come ashore to hunt for meat, of which we have little on the island, and to gather fruits and nuts which do not happen to grow there. If we are lucky, we may take back a few men and women as slaves. I was hunting on the mainland when I was captured."

"But suppose you should escape——"

"I shall not escape," he replied.

"But just suppose you should. Would you be able to find Ruva again? Might it not have floated away?"

"Yes; but I would find my canoe. If I could not find it, I would build another one; and then I would follow Ruva. It moves very slowly in a slow current. I should follow it and overtake it."

The ants did not bother us except to feed us, and time hung heavily upon our hands. I learned to eat the food which they forced down me without vomiting, and I recall that I slept many times. The monotony became almost insupportable; and I suggested to U-Val that, as long as we were going to be killed anyway, we might as well be killed trying to make our escape. U-Val didn't agree with me.

"I am going to die too soon, anyway," he said. "I don't want to hasten it."

Once a winged ant came into the room, and all the other ants gathered around it. They were all feeling the newcomer and one another with their sensitive antennae.

"Oh ho!" exclaimed U-Val. "One of us is about to die."

"How do you know? What do you mean?"

"The one with the wings has come to select a meal, possibly for the queen, possibly for the warriors; and as we are the only prisoners here, it will be one of us or maybe both."

"I am going to fight," I said.

"What with?" he demanded. "That little stone knife? You might kill a few of them; but it would do you no good. There are too many of them."

"I am going to fight," I repeated, doggedly. "They can't murder me without a battle."

"All right," said U-Val, "if you want to fight, I'll fight too; but it won't do us any good."

"It will do me some good to kill a few of these hellish creatures."

After the winged ant had conferred awhile with its fellows, it came over to us and felt over our entire bodies with its antennae, sometimes pinching our flesh lightly with its mandibles. When it had completed its examination it returned again to confer with the other ants.

"I think you are the fattest and the tenderest," said U-Val.

"You mean you hope so."

"Well, of course, I do not wish to see you die," he said; "but neither do I wish to die myself. However, whichever one they choose, I will fight, as you suggest."

"We can at least get a little revenge by killing one or two of them," I said.

"Yes, that will be something," he replied.

The winged ant left the chamber, and after awhile two of the great soldier ants came in. Again there was a conference of antennae, after which one of the ants led the two soldiers over toward us. It went directly to U-Val and touched him with its antennae.

"It is I," said U-Val.

"If they start to take you away, use your knife; and I will help you," I said.

The ant that had brought the soldiers over to us went away about its business; and then one of the soldiers advanced upon U-Val with opened mandibles.

"Now!" I called to U-Val, as I drew my stone knife.

⩣ 21 ⩤

AS THE warrior ant was about to seize U-Val, he struck at it with his stone knife severing one of its antennae; and at the same instant I leaped upon it from the side, driving my knife into its abdomen. Instantly it turned upon me, trying to seize me in its mandibles; and U-Val struck again, piercing one of its eyes, while I drove my knife home several times in quick succession. The creature rolled over upon its side, writhing and floundering; and we had to beat a hasty retreat to escape the menace of its powerful legs.

The other warrior ant approached its fellow and felt of it; then it backed away, apparently confused;

but in some way it must have communicated with the other ants in the room for immediately they became very excited, running hither and thither but finally converging upon us in a body.

They were a menacing sight. Their utter silence, their horrible blank, expressionless faces carried a sinister menace that is indescribable.

The creatures were almost upon us when there was an interruption from above. Rocks and debris commenced to fall into the chamber from the ceiling; and, glancing up, I saw that something was tearing at the opening and enlarging it rapidly. One of the honey-pots fell to the floor and burst. A long, furry nose was thrust through the opening in the ceiling, and a slender tongue reached down into the chamber, licking up the ants, as more of the ceiling fell in to add further to the confusion which suddenly seized them. They seemed to forget us entirely; and immediately there was a scramble for the opening leading into the tunnel. The ants crawled over one another and jammed the entrance in panic; and constantly the great tongue licked them up, and more of the ceiling fell in.

U-Val and I ran and crouched close against the wall at the far side of the chamber in an effort to escape the falling boulders, while above us the beast tore away with powerful claws as it sought to enlarge the opening.

The long, powerful tongue sought out every corner of the room. Twice it passed over our bodies; but each time it discarded us as it sought for more ants. When there were no more left, the tongue and the head were withdrawn from the great hole that the creature had made in the top of the ant hill.

The chamber was filled with debris that reached to the edge of the great rent in the ceiling. It formed an avenue of escape; and there was not an ant in sight.

"Come," I said to U-Val, "let's get out of here before the ants recover from their confusion."

Together we scrambled up the pile of rubble; and when we stood again in the open there was not an ant in sight; but there was a colossal ant bear, as large as an elephant, digging at another part of the hill. In appearance the creature was almost identical with the South American ant bear of the outer crust but highly specialized as to size, because of the enormous ants upon which it fed.

Perry and I had often speculated upon the amazing similarity between many of the animals of Pellucidar and of the outer crust; and Perry had formulated a theory to explain this which I believe is based on quite sound reasoning.

It has been quite clearly demonstrated that at some time in the past, tropical conditions existed at what are now the Arctic regions; and it is Perry's belief that at this time animals passed freely through the polar opening from the outer crust to the inner world; but be that as it may there was a great ant bear, and to it we owed our lives.

Animated by a common impulse, U-Val and I hastened away from the ant hills and down toward the ocean; and I may say that I never left any place before with a greater sense of relief, not even the village of Meeza, King of the Jukans.

At the edge of the surf, U-Val stopped and gazed out across the ocean, shading his eyes with his hand as he strained them into the distance.

As I followed his gaze I was suddenly struck with

a change in the seascape since last I had seen it.

"That is strange," I said.

"What?" demanded U-Val.

"The last time I looked out across this water, there were islands out there. I saw them distinctly. I could not have been mistaken."

"You were not mistaken," said U-Val. "They were The Floating Islands, of which Ruva is one."

"And now you will never see your own country again," I said. "That is too bad."

"Of course I shall see it again," said U-Val, "that is, if I am not killed as I am going to it."

"But even if you had a boat, how would you know in what direction to go?" I asked.

"I will always know where Ruva lies, no matter where it is. I do not know how. I simply know." He pointed. "Beyond the range of our vision it lies directly there."

Now here was a new phase of that amazing homing instinct which is inherent to all Pellucidarians. Here was a man whose country floated around aimlessly, possibly, upon a great ocean, at the mercy of tide and current and wind; yet no matter where it might be

U-Val, given means of transportation, could go directly to it, or at least so he thought. I wondered if it were true.

The point on the coast at which U-Val had left his canoe was in the direction that I had intended going; so I went with him to look for it.

"If it is not there," he said. "I shall have to build another; and while I am doing it, Ruva will have drifted much farther. I hope that I shall find my boat."

Find it he did, where he had hidden it among some tall reeds in a tiny inlet.

U-Val said that he had to make a number of spears before attempting the long journey in search of Ruva. He said that he should probably be attacked many times by sea monsters during the trip; and the only weapon that he could use against them with any degree of success was a long spear.

"We shall have to have many of them," he said.

" 'We'?" I repeated. "I am not going with you."

He looked astonished. "You are not?" he demanded. "But where will you go? You have told me that you don't know how to find your way to your own country. You had much better come with me."

"No," I said. "I know that Sari does not lie out in the middle of an ocean and that if I went there I should never find it; whereas, if I stick to the sea-shore, I may eventually come to it, if this is, as I think, the ocean near which it lies."

"It is not as I had planned," he said; and I thought that his tone was a little sullen.

"I'll stay with you until you shove off," I told him, "for I have to make more weapons for myself—a short spear, a bow, and some arrows."

He asked me what bow-and-arrows were, as he had never heard of them. He thought that they might be handy and in some ways better than a spear.

Once again I set to work making weapons. It may seem to you that I had very bad luck with my weapons, constantly losing them as I did; but making them entailed very little work as they were most crudely done. However, they had always answered my purpose; and, after all, that is the only thing that matters.

U-Val kept reverting to the subject of my accompanying him. He seemed absolutely set upon it and was continually trying to persuade me to change my mind.

I couldn't understand why he was so insistent for he had never given the slightest indication of harboring any affection for me. Accident had thrown us, two alien people, together; and about the most that one might say about it was that we were not unfriendly.

U-Val was a fine-looking chap; and in the bright sunlight he was a deep black with a copper glint. His features were quite regular; and he was, all in all, quite handsome. The first man-like creatures I had seen on Pellucidar, when Perry and I first broke through the crust from the outer world, were black men; but they were arboreal creatures with long tails, and low in the scale of human evolution. U-Val, however, was of an entirely different type and, I should say, fully as intelligent as any of the white race of Pellucidar that I had seen.

After I had finished my weapons, I helped him with the making of his spears as I had promised to stay with him until he sailed. At last, the weapons were completed and the boat stocked with water and food. The former he carried in sections cut from large, bamboo-like plants, which, he maintained, would keep the water fresh indefinitely. His food supply consisted of tubers and nuts, a diet that would be varied by the addition of such fish as he might be able to spear enroute.

When all was ready, he suggested that we sleep before separating so that we might both be fresh for the start of our journeys.

Just before I awoke, I dreamed of Dian. She had taken both my hands in hers; and then, in one of those weird transformations which occur in dreams, she suddenly became a Hartford, Connecticut, policeman, fettering my hands behind me with handcuffs. Just as the lock snapped, I awoke.

I was lying on my side, and U-Val was standing over me. It was a moment before I gathered my wits, and when I did I found that in fact my hands were bound behind my back.

At first I couldn't realize what had happened to me. The recollection of the dream still clung persistently in my mind. But what was U-Val doing in it? He didn't belong in the same picture with a cop from Hartford, Connecticut—and where was the cop? Where was Dian?

Presently my brain cleared, and I realized that I was still alone with U-Val; and that it must have been he who had bound my hands behind my back. But why?

"U-Val," I demanded, "what's the meaning of this?"

"It means that you are going to Ruva with me," he replied.

"But I don't want to go to Ruva."

"That's the reason I bound your hands. Now you'll have to go. You can't do anything about it."

"But why do you want me to come with you?"

U-Val thought for a moment before he answered; then he said, "Well, there's no reason why you shouldn't know, because there's nothing you can do about it. I'm taking you back to Ruva as my slave."

"Where I come from," I said, "you'd almost qualify as a rat."

"What's a rat?" he asked. I had used the English word, which, of course, he did not understand.

"You are—almost. A rat has some redeeming qualities, I suppose; though I don't know just what they are. You have none. You accepted my friendship. Together we suffered imprisonment and faced death. Together we fought against a common enemy for our freedom. Together we escaped. And now you bind me in my sleep, planning to take me back to your country as your slave."

"What's wrong with that?" he demanded. "You are not a Ruvan; therefore, we are enemies. You should be glad that I didn't kill you while you slept. I let you live because a man with slaves is an important man in Ruva. Now that I have a slave I shall be able to get a mate. No woman of Ruva, who is worth having, will mate with a man who has no slaves. It takes a brave man and a fine warrior to capture a slave."

"The way you did?"

"I do not have to tell them how I got you," he said.

"But I can tell them," I reminded him.

"You won't, though," he said.

"And why?"

"Because a man may kill a bad slave."

"My hands will not always be bound behind my back," I said.

"Nevertheless, with my friends, I can kill you, if you tell this about me."

"I shall tell no lies."

"You had better tell nothing. Come! We'll be going. Get up!" He gave me a kick in the ribs. I was furious, but helpless.

It is not easy to get up when your hands are bound behind your back, but with the aid of head, shoulder, and elbow I finally got to one knee and then to my feet.

U-Val pushed me, none too gently, toward his canoe. "Get in," he commanded. I sat down in the bow. U-Val cast off, and took his place in the stern. With his great paddle he headed the frail craft out of the inlet toward the open sea; and thus commenced a journey on an uncharted ocean in a frail craft, without sextant or compass, toward a destination that was constantly shifting its position.

⊰ 22 ⊱

AS I CONTEMPLATED the vast expanse of ocean ahead and the inadequate craft that was supposed to transport us to our elusive destination, I wouldn't have given U-Val a lead nickel for his slave. As a matter of fact, I seemed more of a liability than an asset, for I was merely dead weight that U-Val had to carry; but I was reckoning without full appreciation of U-Val's resourcefulness.

After we had gone about a mile from land, a small saurian rose from the depths; and when his cold, forbidding eyes discovered us, he came for us, his jaws distended, his long neck arched, the water rippling from his sleek body.

He presented a most formidable appearance; and, though not one of the larger species, he was, I knew, fully as formidable as he appeared and quite capable of ending our voyage almost before it was started.

I had encountered these terrible creatures before, and so I knew something of what to expect of blind and senseless ferocity. They are wanton destroyers, killing, apparently, solely for the sake of killing, though I will have to admit that they seem never to be able to satisfy their ravenous hunger, and eat nearly everything they kill.

Bound and helpless in the bow of the canoe, I would fall easy prey to the killer, which would doubtless pluck me out and devour me before finishing U-Val. Such were my thoughts as the saurian bore down upon us. Yet there was that about the situation which offered some compensation even for the loss of my life, and I couldn't resist the temptation to take full advantage of it.

"You are about to lose your slave," I called to U-Val, "and no one will ever know you owned one. Being a rat didn't pay, U-Val."

U-Val made no reply. The saurian was about a

hundred feet away now and coming rapidly, hissing like a leaky steam valve. The canoe was broadside to him.

U-Val swung the craft around, presenting the stern, where he sat, to the charging reptile; then he seized one of the long spears we had made, and stood up.

I hated to admit it; but it certainly seemed that U-Val had plenty of intestinal fortitude, and he unquestionably didn't intend to give up his slave without a struggle.

The saurian came straight for him. U-Val poised his twenty foot spear, and when the creature was within fifteen feet of the boat he drove the point of the weapon deep into the reptile's carcass. It was done with all the skill and assurance of a professional matador giving the *coup de grace* to a bull.

Perhaps half a minute the saurian lashed about in an effort to reach U-Val; but the man, clinging to his end of the spear, skillfully held the canoe in a straight course in front of the beast; so that all its efforts to reach us only succeeded in propelling the craft through the water, until, at last, with a final, convulsive shudder, it rolled over, belly up, dead. The point of U-Val's spear had pierced its heart.

Had it been a more highly organized creature it would have died sooner. It is really astonishing the length of time it takes for perceptions of even mortal injuries to reach the brains of some of the lower orders of Pellucidar. I have seen a lidi painfully wounded in the tail totally unconscious of its hurt for almost a full minute; but then it is sometimes a matter of sixty feet from the tip of a lidi's tail to its minute brain at the far extremity of its huge body.

U-Val dragged the carcass to the side of the canoe and hacked off some of its flesh with his stone knife. Before he had finished, the water was alive with terrible, carnivorous fishes and reptiles attracted by the promise of flesh. As they fought over the remains of the saurian, U-Val seized his paddle and drove the canoe out of further immediate danger as rapidly as he could; then, when we were at a safe distance, he laid aside his paddle and cut the meat of the saurian into thin strips which he strung across one of the spears to dry in the sun.

All this time, U-Val never addressed me. He resumed his paddling, and I curled up under my shelter and fell asleep. Let the master paddle for the shore, I thought dreamily just before I lost consciousness.

When I awoke we were out of sight of land. U-Val was paddling steadily with long, powerful strokes, yet seeming utterly tireless. I must have slept for a long time as land a hundred miles away, possibly a hundred and fifty, would have been visible, as the atmosphere was quite clear. At a rough guess, I should say that U-Val must have been paddling for at least fifteen hours—paddling a twenty foot canoe heavily laden. The strength and endurance of the men of the maritime tribes of Pellucidar is astounding.

The canoe was beautifully designed for speed; and, although hewn from a single tree trunk, was extremely light. The bottom was a trifle more than an inch thick, and from there the thickness tapered to to the gunwales which flared outward to a breadth of four inches. The hull was as smooth as glass, and how they achieved such perfection with the crude implements at their command is a mystery to me.

The wood of the tree from which the canoe was hewn is as tough as wrought iron and very oily. To this latter characteristic is partially attributable the ease with which it glides through the water.

The cargo was stowed amidships and covered with the enormous leaves of a palm-like jungle tree. Each of us had shelters made of these leaves which we could lower quickly when it was necessary. At least, U-Val could lower his; but with my hands bound, I, of course, could not lower mine; nor was there any occasion for me to do so. It is always desirable to be protected from the eternal noonday sun, which has long since burned me to the color of a South Sea Islander.

Shortly after the encounter with the saurian, U-Val laid aside his paddle and came forward to where I sat.

"I am going to free your hands, slave," he said. "You will paddle. You will also help me if we are attacked by any of the larger beasts, such as an azdyryth. You will remain always at this end of the canoe. If you come aft, I'll kill you. I shall only tie you up when I wish to sleep. Otherwise, you might kill me."

"You need not tie me while you sleep," I replied. "I will not kill you then, I promise you. We might be attacked while you slept, and then you wouldn't have time to free me. You may need me, badly, you know."

He thought this over for awhile, and at last he agreed that I was right. "Anyway, it wouldn't do you any good to kill me," he said, "for you might never find your way to land again. The Bandar Az reaches farther than any man knows. Perhaps it has no farther shore. That is what many men think. No, you would not dare to kill me."

"I have promised that I will not kill you while you sleep," I replied; "but some day I will kill you—not because you made me your prisoner, though, under the circumstances, that is reason enough in itself; but because you kicked me while I lay bound and helpless. For that, U-Val, I will kill you."

He had finished removing the bonds from my wrists; and he returned to his seat without comment-

ing on what I had said, but he had something else
to say.

"There is a paddle forward under the pangos
leaves. Take it, slave, and paddle," he commanded.
"I shall steer."

At first I was minded to refuse; but I saw no good
reason for it, as I needed the exercise badly after
lying so long in the ant hill, stuffed with grain and
honey; so I took up the paddle and went to work.

"Faster!" commanded U-Val. "Faster, slave!"

I told him where to go; and it wasn't Heaven,
either.

"What you need is a beating," he growled; and
with that he started forward with a length of bamboo
in his hand. I dropped the paddle and picked up
one of the long spears.

"Come on, U-Val!" I cried. "Come on and beat
your slave."

"Put down that spear!" he commanded. "That is
no way for a slave to act. Don't you know anything?"

"I don't know how to be a slave," I admitted. "At

least not to a stupid clout like you. If you had any brains, neither one of us would have to paddle. But why don't you come on up here and beat me? I'd like nothing better than to have you try it."

"Put down that spear, and I will," he said.

"Go back and sit down. Go way back and sit down."

He thought the matter over for awhile, and then evidently decided that if he wanted a live slave or a live master he'd better not push the matter too far; so he went aft again and sat down. So did I, but I didn't paddle.

After awhile he picked up his paddle and went to work, but he was quite surly about it. He was not a very bright person, and evidently he was much concerned about what attitude he should take with a recalcitrant slave, never having had a slave before. But what troubled him most was the suggestion I had made that it was stupid for either of us to paddle.

Finally he broke a long silence by saying, "How could we get anywhere without paddling?"

"By sailing," I replied.

He didn't know what I meant, for there is no

equivalent for sailing in the Pellucidarian language. They just haven't reached that stage in progress. They have stone weapons; and they have learned to make fire, but sailing is something their greatest minds have not, as yet, conceived.

We had a steady wind blowing in the direction U-Val had been paddling; so I saw no reason why we shouldn't take advantage of it, for after all paddling under a noonday sun is no joke.

"What is sailing?" he asked.

"I'll show you. Let me have some of that grass rope you have back there."

"What for?" he demanded.

"Give it to me, and I'll show you. Do you want the canoe to go without paddling, or do you want to paddle? It makes no difference to me because I don't intend to paddle, anyway."

"Listen!" he fairly shouted. "I'm sick of this. Don't you know you're my slave? Don't you know you have to paddle if I tell you to? If you don't paddle, I'll come up and tie you up again and give you a good beating—that's what you need."

"I won't paddle, and you won't beat me. If you

come up here, I'll run a spear through you. Now, toss that rope up and quit being a fool. I want to show you something that'll save you a lot of hard work."

He kept on paddling away, and the scowl on his face would have soured cream. The wind freshened. The canoe rose and fell as it topped the waves and dropped into the troughs. The sun beat down out of a cloudless sky. U-Val was dripping sweat from every pore. At last he laid down his paddle; and, without a word, tossed a coil of rope forward to me.

It wasn't easy to rig a sail alone; but finally, with spears, a couple of lengths of bamboo, the grass rope, and several pangos leaves from the cargo covering, I fashioned a spread of "canvas" that would take the wind. Instantly the canoe shot forward, cutting the waves in brave style.

"Steer!" I called to U-Val. He started to paddle.

"Don't paddle!" I told him. "Put your paddle in the water astern with the edge up; then turn it first one way and then another until you learn what happens; then you will know how to steer."

He could steer all right, but he had been so surprised to see the canoe move forward without paddling that he had become confused. Presently, however, he was steering; but he didn't say anything for a long time.

At last he asked, "Suppose the wind should blow from another direction?"

"Then you'd have to paddle," I told him. "If you had a boat properly constructed you could sail almost into the wind."

"Could you build such a canoe?" he asked.

"I could show you how to."

"You will be a very valuable slave," he said. "You will show me how to build a canoe that will go without paddling."

"As long as I am a slave, I'll show you nothing," I replied.

⊰ 23 ⊱

I DON'T know how long that voyage lasted. I slept many times, but I rigged up a contraption of spears and ropes so designed that U-Val could not approach without awakening me.

The wind held steadily in the same quarter. The canoe slipped through the water like a living thing, and U-Val was so pleased that he was almost decent. Several times—yes, many times—we were attacked by the fierce denizens of this paleolithic sea; but I had recovered my bow-and-arrows from beneath the cargo covering; and my arrows, together with U-Val's spears, always succeeded in averting the sudden death with which the terrible jaws of these horrific monsters threatened us.

The monotony of that voyage was the one thing about it which impressed me, and which I shall never forget. Even the hideous saurians rushing to attack us made less of an impression upon my mind than the deadly monotony of that vast expanse of horizonless water that stretched in all directions about us beyond the limits of human vision. Never a smudge of smoke from some distant steamer, for there were no steamers. Never a sail, for there were no sails—just empty ocean.

And then, at long last, I sighted land dead ahead. At first it was just a dark haze in the distance, but I knew that it could be nothing but land. I called U-Val's attention to it; but, though he strained his eyes, he could not discern it. I was not greatly surprised, as I had long since discovered that my eyesight was much keener than that of the Pellucidarians. Perhaps the possession of a marvelous homing instinct lessened the need of long range vision for them. They had never had to strain their eyes into the distance searching for familiar landmarks. That is just a theory of my own. It may be quite wrong. But this I will say for them: their hearing and their sense of smell were far keener than mine.

Not being able to see what I saw, U-Val insisted that I saw nothing. Human nature has not changed at all since the Stone Age.

We sailed on; and even though U-Val saw no land he held our course straight for that distant smudge that slowly took more definite shape, a fact which assured me that it must be the floating island of Ruva. Again, as I had a thousand times before, I marveled at that amazing instinct, inexplicable alike to those who possess it and to those who do not. How can it be explained? I haven't even a theory.

At last, U-Val saw the land ahead. "You were right," he admitted grudgingly. "There is land ahead; and it is Ruva, but I don't understand how you could have seen it so much sooner than I."

"That is quite easily explained," I replied.

"How?" he demanded.

"I can see farther than you can."

"Nonsense!" he snapped. "No one can see any farther than I."

What was the use of arguing with a mind like that? Anyway, I had something more important to discuss with him. I fitted an arrow to my bow.

"Why are you doing that?" he demanded, glancing quickly around. "There is nothing to shoot."

"There is you," I said.

For a moment he didn't quite grasp the implication. When he did, he reached for a spear.

"Don't touch it!" I commanded, "or I'll put an arrow through your heart."

He let his hand drop to his side. "You wouldn't dare," he said without much conviction.

"And why not? I can see land ahead, and I can reach it without any help from you."

"It would do you no good. My people would kill you."

"Perhaps, and perhaps not," I countered. "I should tell them that I am your friend and that you sent me to Ruva to get a rescue party to come to the mainland to save you because you are being held a prisoner. If they are all as stupid as you, they will believe me; and they will take me back to the mainland to guide them to you. When we reach there, I shall pretend to go alone to spy upon the tribe that captured you; and I shall not come back. That is the last they will ever see of me."

"But you wouldn't kill me, David," he plead. "We have been friends. We fought side by side. When I could have killed you, I spared your life."

"But you kicked me in the belly when I was bound and helpless," I reminded him.

"I am sorry," he wailed; "and, anyway, I didn't kick you very hard. Oh, please don't kill me, David. Let me live, and I will do everything I can for you."

"Well, I am not going to kill you, because for some reason I couldn't bring myself to kill a helpless man in cold blood if there were any way to avoid it without jeopardizing my own life; so I will make you a proposition. If I spare your life, you must promise to take me among your people, not as a slave but as a friend whom you will protect from other members of your tribe; and at the first opportunity you will help me return to the mainland."

"I promise," he said, eagerly. A little too eagerly, I thought. I should have killed him then; and I knew it, but I couldn't bring myself to the point of murder.

"Very well, see that you keep your promise," I said, laying aside my bow.

As we neared the floating island of Ruva it appeared as low, level land, thickly grown with trees. It floated low in the water, its upper surface scarcely more than five feet above the waterline; and nowhere could I detect any sign of hills. The coast directly in view was irregular, being broken by small inlets or bays; and into one of these U-Val steered our craft. I took down our sail, and he paddled to shore.

It was good to feel ground beneath my feet again and to be able to stretch and move about.

U-Val made the canoe fast to a tree; and then, cupping his hands, voiced a high, piercing call. Then he listened. Presently, from far away came an answering cry.

"Come!" said U-Val. "They are by the fishing hole;" and he started off toward the interior along a well defined trail that wound through the forest.

The trees, of no great size, grow close together

They are of a species I had never seen before, as soft and spongy as some varieties of cactus but without spines or thorns. It is these trees which really not only make The Floating Islands, of which Ruva is one, but also make them a fit abode for human beings. The roots of the trees, closely interlaced, keep the islands from disintegrating and form a natural basket which holds the soil in which the vegetation grows. The trees also furnish a portion of the food supply of the islanders and all of their supply of fresh water, which they can obtain at any time by either tapping the bole of a tree or cutting off a limb. The tender young shoots are edible, and the fruit of the tree is one of the principal staples of food. There is little other vegetation on the islands, and little need for other. Some long grass grows among the trees and there are several parasitic vines which sport gorgeous blooms. A few varieties of birds live on the islands, affording the inhabitants a little variety in diet from the staple tree-food and fish, as they eat both their flesh and their eggs.

We had walked about a mile when we came to an

area that had been partially cleared. A few scattered trees had been left, probably for the purpose of holding the soil together with live roots. In the center of the clearing a hole had been cut, possibly a hundred feet in diameter, forming a small pool. Some fifty people of both sexes and all ages were gathered in the clearing. Several of them stood beside the pool with their spears poised, waiting for a fish to swim within striking distance. The fishes must have learned from experience what would happen to them if they swam too close to the shoreline, for the center of the pool, out of range of a spear-thrust, fairly teemed with fish. Occasionally a foolish or unwary individual would swim within range, when instantly he would be impaled upon a barbed spearhead. The skill of these spearmen was most uncanny—they never missed; but because of the wariness of the fish, their catches were few.

As U-Val and I entered the clearing, the first man to notice us said, "U-Val has returned!" Then every eye was turned upon us; but there was no enthusiastic greeting for the returned prodigal.

A big fellow came toward us. "You have brought back a slave," he said. It was not a question, merely a statement of fact.

"I am not a slave," I rejoined. "U-Val and I were imprisoned together. We fought together. We escaped together; and so, in honor, U-Val could not make me his slave."

"If you are not a slave, you are an enemy," replied the man; "and enemies we kill."

"I would come here as a friend," I said. "There is no reason why we should be enemies. As a matter of fact, I can be a very valuable friend."

"How?" he demanded.

"I can show you how to build canoes that will travel without paddling," I replied; "and I can show you how to catch the fish in the middle of the pool, which you are unable to reach with your spears."

"I don't believe you can do either of those things," he said, "for if they could have been done, we could have done them. We know all there is to know about canoes and fishing. No one can teach us anything new."

I turned to U-Val. "Didn't I make your canoe go without paddling?" I demanded.

U-Val nodded. "Yes, it went even faster than I could paddle; but I can show them how to do that."

"Yes," I replied; "but you can only show them how it is done when the wind is directly behind you; but I can show them how to build canoes in which they can travel no matter in what direction the wind is blowing. That, you cannot do."

"Is that true, U-Val?" asked the man.

"Yes, Ro-Tai, it is true," replied U-Val.

"And can he catch fish from the middle of the pool?"

"That, I do not know."

Ro-Tai turned to me. "If you can do these things at all," he said, "you can do them just as well if you are a slave."

"But I won't do them if I am a slave. I won't show you how to, either."

"You will, or we'll kill you," snapped Ro-Tai.

"If you kill me, you'll never learn how to do it," I reminded him.

While we had been talking, a number of men had congregated about us, interested listeners. Now one of them spoke up. "We should accept this man as a friend, Ro-Tai," he said, "on condition that he teaches us these things."

"Yes," said another, "Ul-Van has spoken words of wisdom. I do not believe that the stranger can do these things; and, if he cannot, we can either make him a slave or kill him."

Quite a discussion ensued in which everybody took part. Some were opposed to accepting a stranger as a friend; but the majority of them agreed with Ul-Van, who seemed to me to be by far the most intelligent member of the company.

Finally, someone said, "Ro-Tai is chief. Let him decide."

"Very well," said Ro-Tai, "I shall decide;" then he turned to me. "Go now and catch a fish from the center of the pool."

"I shall have to make some preparation," I said. "I haven't everything that I need."

"You see," remarked one of the dissenters, "that

he is unable to do it. He is trying to gain time so that he may escape."

"Nonsense," said Ul-Van. "Let him make his preparations, and then if he fails it will be time enough to say that he cannot do it."

Ro-Tai nodded. "Very well," he said, "let him make his preparations; but you, Ul-Van, must stay with him always, to see that he does not try to escape."

"If he cannot do it, he shall be my slave," said U-Val, "for I brought him here."

"If he can't do it, he'll be killed," said Ro-Tai, "for trying to make fools of us."

As soon as I was turned over to Ul-Van, I told him that I wanted a light, stout cord about thirty feet long.

"Come with me," he said; and led me off along another trail beyond the pool. Presently we came to a second clearing in which were the sleeping shelters of the tribe. They were small, beehive huts, entirely covered with large leaves. At the bottom of each hut was a single opening, and into one of these Ul-

Van crawled, emerging presently with a length of the braided grass rope such as I had seen in U-Val's canoe. It was far too heavy for my purpose; but as it was made up of a number of smaller strands braided together, I saw that by unbraiding it I could get a single strand that would answer my purpose. This, he permitted me to do; and I finally had a light cord about forty feet long.

Thus equipped, I returned to the pool. Here I fastened one end of the cord securely to the butt of an arrow and tied the other end around my right wrist; then I stepped to the end of the pool and fitted my arrow to the bow.

Every eye was upon me now as I stepped to the edge of the pool. Milling around in the center of the pool, leaping out of the water, were literally hundreds and hundreds of fish; but none of them approached within spear length of the shore.

I coiled the slack of the rope carefully at my feet, raised the bow and drew the arrow back its full length. I was very nervous, and well I might have been, for I had never tried this thing before; and I did not know if the arrow could carry true with the weight of the rope trailing behind it, and my life depended upon success.

I took careful aim at a spot where the fish were thickest. The bow twanged and the arrow sped straight for its mark. A fish jumped into the air and sounded. The rope payed out rapidly. I braced my feet and prepared for the shock; and when it came I was almost jerked into the pool, but I managed to keep my footing.

I let the fish play for awhile without endeavoring to draw him in, for I was none too sure of the strength of my line, even though it had withstood the first great shock. I wanted to tire him, and every time that there was a little slack in the rope I pulled it in. Finally the struggling ceased, and the fish floated to the surface, belly up. I pulled it ashore and handed it to Ro-Tai, who immediately demanded that I make bows and arrows for every warrior of the tribe. Right there we ran into a snag. There was no growth on Ruva suitable for making bows. The result was that I was kept busy shooting fish.

Ro-Tai had to admit that I had taught them something, and his attitude toward me relaxed a little; but

U-Val was still pretty sore at me. He wanted me as his slave, and he wanted all the credit for what I had done. Ul-Van told me that U-Val was very unpopular and that I was fortunate in not having him for a master.

The fish that I caught they cleaned and smoked, and when they thought they had a sufficient supply Ro-Tai insisted that I show them how to build a canoe that would travel through the water without paddling.

Immediately I was faced by an insurmountable obstacle. No trees suitable for canoe building grew upon Ruva or any of the other floating islands. All of their canoes had been built upon the mainland where the proper wood could be found. To build a canoe was a terrific undertaking, necessitating an expedition in which some twenty or thirty men were often absent from Ruva for a hundred sleeps or more.

The canoes would be roughly hewn on the mainland and then towed to Ruva, where the long and arduous job of finishing was completed.

These canoes remained in families for generations. Ul-Van told me that his had been in his family for ten generations, at least. They are passed on from the father to the eldest son.

As the women and children seldom leave the islands, only enough canoes are needed to carry the men. A new canoe is built only when the number of men in the tribe exceeds the carrying capacity of the canoes they have; and this, Ul-Van told me, seldom occurs more than a couple of times during the lifetime of a man, as the casualties among the warriors just about balance the birth-rate of males.

≥ 24 ≥

I SHALL not bore you with a detailed description
of my attempts to convert one of their canoes into a
sailboat. I discovered, after considerable experimenting, that I could harden the wood of the native
trees over a bed of hot coals; and, with this make-
shift material, I constructed a keel and an outrigger.
My only tools were some large shells with sharp
edges, a stone knife, a stone chisel, and a hammer of
stone. Fortunately for me, the wood was very soft
and I worked it into shape before hardening it. I
made the keel with a broad flange at the top and
fastened it to the bottom of the canoe with fire-

hardened, wooden pegs which I knew would expand when wet. For my mast, I spliced lengths of bamboo to the proper height and then bound three of these together with grass cord. The sail was perhaps the most difficult problem; but I solved it by building a primitive loom and teaching a couple of the women how to weave, using a long, tough grass.

While I was working on the canoe, I became pretty well acquainted with the members of the tribe and their customs. There were about forty families on this island, averaging about four members to the family. There were also twenty-five or thirty slaves —men and women from the white races of the mainland. These slaves attended to practically all of the manual labor; but their life was not a difficult one, and, for the most part, they were well treated.

The men are monogamous and very proud of their blood-line. Under no circumstances will they mate with a white, as they consider the white race far inferior to theirs. I could never quite accustom myself to this reversal of the status of the two races from what I had always been accustomed to; but it really was not as difficult as it might appear, for I must admit that the blacks treated us with far greater toleration here than our dark-skinned races are accorded on the outer crust. Perhaps I was getting a lesson in true democracy.

The canoe upon which I had been working had been drawn up on the seashore about half a mile from the village. Usually, there were a number of villagers hanging around watching me; and Ul-Van was always with me, having been detailed by Ro-Tai to keep a watch on me and prevent me from escaping.

Once, while Ul-Van and I were alone, I saw a canoe approaching in the distance, and called Ul-Van's attention to it. At first he couldn't see it; but when it came closer, and he could recognize it as a canoe, he showed considerable excitement.

"They are probably Ko-vans," he said. "It is a raiding party."

"There are three more canoes coming into sight now behind the first one," I told him.

"That is bad," said Ul-Van. "We must return to the village at once and warn Ro-Tai."

When Ul-Van had reported to Ro-Tai, the latter

sent boys to the fishing pool and to other parts of the island where he knew his warriors to be; and soon all were congregated in the village.

The women and children were sent into the huts; the men stood about nervously, an unorganized crowd presenting a fine target for the spears of the enemy.

"You are not going to remain here, are you?" I asked Ro-Tai.

"This is our village. We shall remain here and defend it," he replied.

"Why don't you go out and meet them?" I asked. "You could take them by surprise. Send a scout out to see what trail they are taking and then hide your warriors on either side of it; then when the Ko-vans walk into your trap, you can fall upon them in force from both sides. They will be surprised and disorganized, and those whom you do not kill will run back to their canoes as fast as they can go. It is not necessary for you to let them reach your village at all."

"All my life, I have fought when raiders came,"

replied Ro-Tai with dignity; "and I, and my father, and his father before him, have always held the warriors in the village to await attack."

"That doesn't make it right," I said. "As a matter of fact, you have always been doing it in the wrong way. If you'll let me have ten men, I'll stop those Ko-Vans before they come anywhere near your village."

"I believe him," said one of the principal men of the village. "He has not deceived us yet."

"His plan is a good one," said Ul-Van.

"Very well," said Ro-Tai. "Take ten men and go and see if you can stop the Ko-vans. The rest of us will remain here to fight with them, if you fail."

"I shall not fail," I said; then I selected Ul-Van and nine other men, and together we started back toward the ocean. I sent one man ahead to reconnoiter, with orders to report back to me as soon as he had discovered what trail the Ko-vans took after they landed.

"They will take this trail," said Ul-Van. "They always do."

"Do they raid you often?" I asked.

"Yes," he replied. "They were here only a few

sleeps before you came. They killed several of our warriors and stole some of our slaves. Among them was a woman slave that belonged to me. I did not like to lose her for she was very beautiful, and my mate was very fond of her. She said that she was an Amozite, and I have heard from other slaves that the women of Amoz are considered very beautiful. She told my woman that she and her mate lived in a country called Sari."

"What was her name?" I asked.

Before Ul-Van could reply, my scout came racing back, breathless. "The Ko-vans have landed," he said. "They are coming along this trail."

"How many of them are there?" I asked.

"About twenty," he replied.

I posted my men on either side of the trail, well hidden behind trees. Each of the warriors carried two spears and a stone knife. I told them not to move or to make any sound until I gave the signal; then they were to stand up and each hurl one of his spears, immediately charging in to close quarters with his remaining spear.

I climbed a tree from which I could not only see

my own men but watch the trail for a short distance along which the Ko-vans were approaching, quite oblivious of the fate that awaited them.

I had not long to wait, for presently a hideously painted warrior came into view; and close behind him, in single file, followed the others. They were armed precisely as were the Ruvans—two spears and a stone knife—and they were of the same race of fine-looking blacks. Only in their war-paint did they differ in appearance from the warriors of Ruva.

Silently I fitted an arrow to my bow and waited until the entire file was well within the ambush. I bent the bow and took careful aim. This was savage warfare, warfare of the Stone Age. Of course, we lacked poison gas, and we couldn't drop bombs on women and children and hospitals; but in our own primitive way we could do fairly well; and so I released my arrow, and as it sunk deep into the body of the last man in the file, I gave the signal for the Ruvan warriors to attack.

With savage war cries they rose and hurled their spears. The Ko-vans, taken entirely by surprise, were thrown into confusion to which I added by driving half a dozen more arrows into as many of them in rapid succession.

Eleven of the twenty went down in the first onslaught. The remaining nine turned to flee; but the trail was narrow and blocked by the dead and wounded. The survivors stumbled and fell as they attempted to climb over one another and their dead and dying comrades in their mad effort to escape, with the result that they fell easy prey to the Ruvan warriors who rushed in with fiendish yells and speared them to the last man.

As I dropped from the tree, they were driving their spears into the hearts of the wounded. Not a Ko-van escaped. Not one of my men received even so much as a scratch.

Bearing the weapons of the vanquished, we marched back to the village in triumph.

When the villagers saw us, they looked at us in astonishment. "Was there no fight?" demanded Ro-Tai. "What became of the Ko-vans? Are they following you?"

"The Ko-vans are all dead," said Ul-Van. "There were twenty of them, and we killed them all."

"You killed twenty Ko-vans without losing a man?" demanded Ro-Tai. "Such a thing has never happened before."

"You can thank David," said Ul-Van. "We did only what he told us to do, and we were victorious."

Ro-Tai made no comment. With the others, he listened to the account of the victorious warriors, which lost nothing of glory in the telling; but I will admit that every last man of them gave me full credit.

At last, Ro-Tai spoke. "The warriors of Ruva will feast in celebration of the victory over the Ko-vans. Let the slaves prepare food and tu-mal, that the warriors may drink and be happy. Only the warriors of Ruva shall partake of this feast."

Some of the slaves were detailed to prepare the food and make the tu-mal, an alcoholic drink of some potency. The remaining male slaves were sent to carry the dead Ko-vans to the sea, where they would be thrown to the fierce denizens of the deep.

As soon as I could get Ul-Van's attention I asked him the name of the slave woman who had been captured by the Ko-vans.

"Amar," he said. "That was her name."

I couldn't tell whether I was disappointed or not. From his description, I had thought that it might be Dian, for she was beautiful, she had been born in Amoz, and she had lived with her mate in Sari; but of course many women have been born in Amoz, and many of them have been taken as mates by the men of Sari, and as nearly all Amozite women are beautiful the description might have fitted many besides Dian; and, anyhow, how could Dian be on one of the floating islands?

Three sleeps intervened before the feast was ready, for the tu-mal had to ferment, and special foods had to be prepared, many of which cooked for long periods under ground wrapped in pangos leaves and laid upon hot stones.

I returned to my work upon the canoe, and Ul-Van remained with me. He was still very much elated over our victory, which he said was absolutely unprecedented in the memory of any living Ruvan.

"We not only killed them all, and have all their weapons, but we have four fine canoes in addition. Never, never has anything like this happened; and you are the one who did it, David."

⪥ 25 ⪤

EVER since I had come to Ruva, I had noticed that U-Val hung around a girl called O-Ra. There were several other young bucks after her, but she showed no preference for any of them. I think O-Ra was something of a paleolithic gold-digger. She wanted a man with a slave; and not one of her suitors owned one. Thus a situation was created which did not tend to increase U-Val's love for me. I think he spent a great deal of time doing nothing but hating me. I used to catch him glaring at me, and I think he was trying to screw up his courage to a pitch where he could denounce me and claim me as his slave. His fear of me was purely psychological—an

unreasoning complex—for he had proved in his encounters with the great saurians which had attacked
us during our voyage from the mainland to Ruva
that he was no coward. I think we have all seen
examples of this type of cowardice many times. I
have known men who could face death coolly but
were in mortal terror of some little woman half their
size, and I have known heroes who were afraid of
mice.

Possibly because they didn't like him, the men of
the tribe made U-Val the butt of crude jokes because
of his profitless attention to O-Ra; and I may say that
Stone Age humor is often raw. However, much of it
has come down intact for perhaps a million years to
the present day on the outer crust. I recognized in
many of the paleolithic jokes old friends with which
I had been well acquainted back in Hartford, Connecticut.

Finally the food and tu-mal for the feast were
about ready; and Ro-Tai announced that the warriors would retire to their huts and that after the
sleep the feast would be served. As Ul-Van had
been detailed to keep watch over me, I had to go into

his hut with him; and while I was waiting for sleep to come, I overheard a conversation in a nearby hut. A man was speaking, and he was trying to persuade a woman to enter the hut with him, which would have consummated the simple marriage ceremony of the Ruvans; but the woman was adamant in her refusal.

"No," she said. "I will not mate with a man who has no slave."

"I have a slave," replied the man; and I recognized the voice of U-Val.

The woman laughed, scornfully. "You keep your slave well hidden, U-Val," she said. "What is it—a man or a woman? Or did the brave U-Val capture a little girl?"

"My slave is a great warrior," replied U-Val. "He is the man called David. Did you not see me bring him to the island?"

"But he said that he was your friend, not your slave; and you did not deny it."

"I did not deny it because he had threatened to kill me if I claimed him as my slave."

"When you claim him," said O-Ra, "I will become

your mate, for the man would make a valuable slave."

"Yes," assented U-Val; but there was not much conviction in his tone. He had reason to doubt that I would make a very tractable slave.

"When you have your slave, you may ask me again," said O-Ra; and then she must have gone away, for I heard no more; and presently I fell asleep.

A boy came and awakened us, saying that Ro-Tai was awake and was summoning the warriors to the feast.

I followed Ul-Van out of the hut, and found a place beneath the shade of a tree where I could watch the proceedings. Leaves had been laid on the ground, covering a strip about three feet wide and twenty-five feet long. This was the banquet table, and along the length of it the slaves were piling food and setting great joints of bamboo filled with tu-mal, the warriors arranging themselves along both sides. Ro-Tai, who was standing at the center of one side of the spread, was looking about as though searching for someone. Suddenly his eyes alighted upon me and he called to me.

"Come, David," he said, "and join the other warriors in the feast."

It was then that U-Val spoke up, finding his courage at last. "Slaves do not eat with the warriors of Ruva, Ro-Tai," he said.

"What do you mean?" demanded Ro-Tai.

"I mean that the man, David, is my slave. I captured him on the mainland, and brought him to Ruva. I have let him play at being a free man long enough. Now I claim him as my slave."

There was a rumble of disapproval, and then Ro-Tai spoke. "Even if David were your slave, by his act he has won his liberty; and I, Ro-Tai, the chief of Ruva, give him his liberty, which it is my right to do. I give him his liberty and I make him a warrior of Ruva."

"I shall not feast with a white slave!" exclaimed U-Val; and, turning, he stalked away. He took a few steps and then stopped and wheeled about. "If I cannot have him as my slave, I can at least kill him, for he is an enemy of Ruva, and kill him I shall!"

"Have you forgotten that you ate grain and honey with me in the hill of the giant ants, U-Val?" I called to him. "You had better come and eat now. You can kill me afterward, and you will need the tu-mal to give you courage; but don't forget, U-Val, that I have promised to kill you."

"Why have you promised to kill him?" demanded Ro-Tai.

"Because, while I thought he was my friend, he bound my hands behind me while I slept, and when I awoke he told me that I was his slave; and he kicked me in the ribs while I lay on the ground helpless. It was because of that kick that I promised to kill him."

"You may kill him in self-defense, but not otherwise," said Ro-Tai. "And see that you don't pick a quarrel with him," he added. "I haven't so many warriors that I can afford to lose even one unnecessarily."

Now, at a sign from Ro-Tai, the warriors seated themselves crosslegged upon the ground before the feast. There were no knives or forks but each warrior had two good hands, and each made the most of both of them. There was not much conversation for the feasters were too busy eating and drinking.

The women and children and slaves formed a circle about us, hungrily watching us devour the food. When we were through, they would come and finish what remained.

It was not long before the feasters began to get pretty high on tu-mal, and correspondingly noisy. I drank no tu-mal, and when I had satisfied my hunger I got up and strolled away; and no sooner had I left than U-Val came and seated himself at the feast. As I watched him I saw that he ate very little, but that he was drinking quantities of tu-mal; and I knew then that I must be on my guard.

I wanted to go and work on the canoe, which was nearly completed; but I could not because Ul-Van couldn't go with me. The slaves were all busy; and so I sat apart by myself, for I had learned long since that the less you have to do with the women of primitive men the better you are liked. Many of them even resent an outsider talking to their women; but after awhile O-Ra came over and sat down beside me. While she didn't belong to anybody, she had several suitors; so that a tete-a-tete with her wasn't a particularly healthful occupation. I was compensated for this, however, by the fact that I knew it would make U-Val madder than ever.

"U-Val is going to kill you," she said. "He told me so just before he went to fill up on tu-mal."

"Why are you warning me?" I asked.

"Because I don't like U-Val, and I hope you kill him," she replied; "then he can't bother me any more."

"But you would have become his mate if he had owned a slave," I said. "How could you do that, if you hated him?"

"He could have died suddenly," she said with a smile; "and then I would have owned the slave. After that I could have mated with the man I want; and then I would have had my man and my slave both."

"You would have killed him?" I asked.

She shrugged. "He would have died," she said.

O-Ra was way ahead of her time. She had been born about a million years too soon, or at least on the wrong side of the crust. She had highly advanced ideas for a girl of the Stone Age.

"Well, I hope you get your man, O-Ra," I said; "but I'd hate to be in his sandals."

She laughed, and rose. Then she said excitedly in a whisper, "Here comes U-Val now. I think I'll wait and see the fun."

"I would if I were you," I said, "for somebody is going to be killed. You ought to enjoy that."

U-Val came toward us a little unsteadily. His habitual scowl was even blacker than usual.

"What are you doing trying to steal my woman?" he demanded.

"Is she your woman?" I asked.

"I'll say I'm not," said O-Ra.

"She's going to be," said U-Val, "and anyway no dirty white slave is going to talk to a Ruvan woman while I'm around."

I wasn't going to be tricked into attacking him no matter what he said, for Ro-Tai had made it quite clear that it wouldn't be safe for me to kill him in other than self-defense.

"Why don't you fight, you dirty coward?" he shouted.

By this time the attention of others had been attracted, and members of the tribe were gathering to form a circle about us. Some of the men were pretty drunk, and they urged on first U-Val and then me. Like O-Ra, they wanted to see a fight and a killing. Ro-Tai and Ul-Van were among the spectators.

U-Val was applying to me every vile Pellucidarian epithet that he could recall, and he recalled plenty and most of them were pretty raw—fighting words, if there ever were any.

"What's the matter?" demanded Ul-Van. "Are you afraid of him, David?"

"Ro-Tai told me that I could only kill him in self-defense," I said, "and he hasn't attacked me yet. Words can't kill me; but if I could use my fists on him, that would help some."

"You can use your fists," said Ro-Tai; "but don't either of you draw a weapon."

"You don't care, then, what I do to him just so long as I do it with my hands?" I asked.

Ro-Tai nodded; and with permission granted, I stepped in and planted a right on U-Val's nose. Blood spurted in all directions, and U-Val went practically crazy with rage. He had gone down with the blow, sort of stunned and dazed; but when he re-gained his senses he leaped up and down like a jump-ing-jack, beating his breast and screaming; then he came for me.

I dropped him again with a body blow to the solar plexus. He was a pretty sick man when he staggered to his feet; but when he saw everyone laughing at him, he lost the last shred of his self-control, whipped out his stone knife, and came for me with murder in his eye.

Now was my opportunity. I could kill him now, according to the rules that Ro-Tai had made; but as he came for me I did not draw my own knife. I wanted to be absolutely in the clear, for I knew that if I killed him there would be some that would insist that I pay with my life. They wouldn't like the idea of a white man living among them who had killed a black. He might become too arrogant.

"Your knife! Your knife!" cried Ul-Van. "Draw your knife, David!" But I didn't have to draw my knife yet, and I hoped that I would not have to draw it at all. I knew a great many jujitsu tricks and holds, and I felt that U-Val was in for the surprise of his life.

As he closed with me I used a very simple trick for disarming him, and then I got his head beneath one arm and started whirling him around. He was absolutely helpless. His feet flew off the ground and his body described a circle in the air. Faster and faster I whirled; then suddenly I lifted him and let him go. His body flew completely over the heads of the spectators and lit heavily on the ground beyond.

I hurried through the crowd to his side. He lay with his head bent under, quite motionless. Immediately the crowd followed and formed a new circle about us. I put my ear to U-Val's chest and listened; then I rose and turned toward Ro-Tai.

"He is dead," I said. "You will all bear witness that I killed him in self-defense."

"And with your bare hands!" exclaimed Ul-Van in evident amazement.

"Have slaves take the body down to the ocean," said Ro-Tai; and turning on his heel he walked away.

The fight seemed to have had a sobering effect upon most of the warriors. Some of them gathered around me and felt of my muscles. "You must be very strong," said one.

"It doesn't take a great deal of strength," I said. "It is just in knowing how."

Immediately they wanted to be taught; so I showed them a few of the simpler holds—how to disarm a man attacking with a knife; how to throw a man; how to take a prisoner and force him to accompany you, and at the same time render him helpless to harm you.

When I was through they immediately started practicing on one another, and they were still at it when Ul-Van and I started back to the seashore to go to work upon the canoe.

I was anxious to complete the work as I hoped to be able to use the canoe to sail to the mainland and escape from Ruva.

I had a plan which I proceeded to explain to Ul-Van, although I did not tell him that its real purpose was to permit me to escape.

"When this canoe is finished," I said, "a party of us can sail to the mainland and get a log from which I can make a better boat. We can tow it back to Ruva and do all the work on it here."

"That is a good idea," said Ul-Van; "but we shall

have to wait until the islands float within sight of the mainland."

"Why?" I asked.

"Because we could never find the mainland, otherwise."

"Do you mean to say that you don't know in what direction the mainland lies?"

"Bandar Az is very large," he said, "and the islands are constantly drifting. We never go to the mainland unless we can see it. Of course, it makes no difference then how far Ruva drifts away from us, for Ruva is our homeland; and no matter where it lies, we can always return to it."

"Will it be long before we sight the mainland?" I asked.

"I do not know," he replied. "Occasionally, there are times when babies grow to manhood without ever sighting the mainland; and then there are times when we are in sight of it constantly for hundreds and hundreds of sleeps."

My chances of escape looked pretty slim, if I had to wait for twenty years of outer crust time before we sighted the mainland again. I was pretty blue.

Presently Ul-Van exclaimed jubilantly, "Why, of course, we can reach the mainland! Why didn't we think of it before? Your home is on the mainland. All you would have to do would be to steer a course for your home."

I shook my head. "That is something I could not do. You see, I am not a Pellucidarian. I am from another world, and I could not steer a straight course to my home as you Pellucidarians can."

That seemed very strange to Ul-Van. It was beyond his comprehension.

Another hope was blasted! I seemed now irretrievably doomed to a life of exile upon this floating bit of earth. I might never again see my beloved Sari; never renew my search for Dian the Beautiful.

I worked on in silence upon the canoe. Ul-Van helped me as best he could, for this was work such as a warrior might do. We had not spoken for some time when he said, "Oh, by the way, David, that slave-girl I was telling you about had another name. Amar was a name my mate gave her. Her real name was Dian."

⊱ 26 ⊰

NOW my entire outlook on life changed. I knew definitely where Dian was. I was sure that she was alive, and I had every reason to believe that she was comparatively safe among the Ko-vans, for Ul-Van assured me that they treated their slaves well. But how was I to rescue her? First I would have to reach Ko-va, and that I could not do alone for it had drifted out of sight of Ruva. Usually, Ul-Van said, they were in sight of one another; but some freak of current or wind had separated them. Eventually they would float together again. On occasions they had even touched each other. Formerly the fighting had

been continuous when this occurred; but both tribes
had been so depleted by this constant warfare that,
for many generations, truces had been declared
whenever the two islands approached within spear-
throw of each other.

At last I hit upon a plan, and when we returned to
the village to eat I went directly to Ro-Tai.

"I have a plan," I said, "whereby you may make a
successful raid upon Ko-va. With the loss of the
twenty warriors we killed, their fighting strength has
been weakened; and if you will let me help you plan
the attack, we should be able to recapture all of the
slaves they took from you and doubtless take all of
their slaves, as well."

Ro-Tai was very much interested. He thought the
plan an excellent one and said that he would embark
upon the expedition after the next sleep.

Later, I was talking the matter over with Ul-Van
when a discouraging thought occurred to me.
"How," I asked him, "can you find Ko-va, if you cannot see it, any more than you can find the mainland
when it is out of sight, for Ko-va is not your home?"

"Some of our women were born on Ko-va," he said,

"and captured by us. We will take one of them with us in one of the canoes, and she will direct our passage."

"How did the Ko-vans who came to raid Ruva find the island?" I asked.

"Unquestionably, at least one of them was born on Ruva," replied Ul-Van, "and doubtless stolen in a raid while he was a small child. We often capture Ko-van boys and raise them. among us as our own warriors for the same purpose. It happened that the last two we had were killed in a recent raid; but we have several Ko-van women."

It seemed to me an eternity before the expedition was prepared to set out; but at last all was in readiness and fifty warriors manned five canoes, one of which was that which I had converted into a lateen rigged outrigger.

Ro-Tai, the chief, and Ul-Van were in this canoe with me; and we had with us a woman who had been born on Ko-va to point the way.

I was not a little concerned as to the success of my venture. I had wanted to experiment with my craft before setting forth upon this considerable voyage, but Ro-Tai would not hear of it. Now that all was ready, he wanted to get started without further delay.

I did not know what speed I could attain and there was a question as to whether the paddle-driven canoes might outdistance us. Also, I was not at all sure as to the seaworthiness of my craft. I was fearful that a good gust of wind might capsize it, for it carried considerable canvas.

The Ruvans were still skeptical about the possibility of making a canoe move through the water without paddles. Fifty pair of eyes were on me as I raised the sail and took my place in the stern with the steering paddle. Gradually the boat got under way with a brisk breeze. The warriors in the other canoes bent to their paddles; and the little armada was under way.

"It moves!" exclaimed Ro-Tai in an awe-struck tone.

"It is pulling away from the other canoes," said Ul-Van.

"Will wonders never cease!" exclaimed one of the older men. "What will they think of next? To think that I should live to see a thing like this!"

The warriors in the other canoes were paddling

furiously, but still we drew away from them. I sailed on, occasionally looking back to note the position of the other canoes; and when I thought we were separated almost too far for safety, I brought the canoe into the wind and waited.

We were a savage-looking band, for the Ruvans had donned their war-paint and were hideously decorated. They had even insisted upon painting me; and when Ul-Van got through with me I could have passed for a full-blooded Ruvan, for he had succeeded in smearing every inch of my body with pigments of one color or another. The canoes were well stocked with spears, each warrior having brought three; and I had made for myself an additional supply of arrows and one of the short, javelin-like spears which I prefer.

I discussed with Ro-Tai his plan of attack when we should have landed on Ko-va. He said that they would do as they had always done—march in a body straight to the village which lay in the center of the island. If the Ko-vans chanced to have seen us approach, they would be ready for us. If not, we might take them partially by surprise. I didn't like this plan at all, and finally persuaded him to adopt one which I felt certain would assure us far greater success and which I explained to him in detail. He acceded with some reluctance, and he acceded at all solely because of the success I had had in our skirmish with the Kovans who had come to raid Ruva.

I was the first to sight the island, which was similar in all respects to Ruva except that it was a little larger. As we approached it we saw no sign of life; and I was in hope that we might be able to surprise the village, for my plan of attack would prove far more successful in such an event.

I came to a short distance from the island and lay to waiting for the other canoes to overtake us. Ul-Van and I lowered the sail, and the warriors shipped their paddles; and when the other canoes came abreast of us we all moved in together toward the shore.

When we had disembarked, Ro-Tai asked me to explain my plan of attack to the entire company; and when I had done so, we started into the forest in a long, thin line which gradually opened out as we approached the village. I took a position in the center of the line; Ro-Tai in the center of the left wing; Ul-Van in the center of the right wing. We kept the men close enough together so that they could see and pass on hand signals, which I explained to them and which were very simple. I sent one scout ahead to the village with explicit instructions as to what he was to do.

We moved forward in absolute silence, and when we had advanced about two miles my scout returned to me. He told me that the village was but a short distance ahead; that he had reached the edge of the clearing, and from what he could see he believed that the warriors were sleeping or away, for he saw only women, children, and slaves outside the huts.

I now gave the signal to start the enveloping movement, and it was passed on to right and left by hand signals. The center of the line moved forward now very slowly while the wings curved inward as they advanced more rapidly, the idea being to entirely surround the village before attacking.

When those in the center of the line reached a point where they could see the clearing, they lay down and hid; but always they kept in sight of the warrior next to them. Finally, the signal that I awaited came. It meant that the two wings had joined on the opposite side of the village.

So far, not a Ko-van was aware that an enemy was upon the island.

Now I gave the signal to charge. It was simply a war cry that was taken up by all the Ruvan warriors as, simultaneously, we dashed toward the village. The women and children, terrified, started to run first in one direction and then in another; but always they found Ruvan warriors blocking their escape.

Now the Ko-van warriors came crawling from their huts, heavy-eyed with sleep. Taken wholly by surprise, they fell easy prey to our spear-men. Only a few of them fell before the others surrendered.

I had expected to see ruthless slaughter; but such was not the case. As Ro-Tai explained to me afterward, if they killed all the Ko-vans they would have no one to raid for slaves and women; and even now, in victory, he exacted but little tribute. He demanded the slaves that had been stolen from Ruva and an equal number of Ko-van slaves, as well as three young boys who would be brought up as Ruvans.

My first concern was to look for Dian; but she was not among the slaves who were in the village. I questioned the chief, and he told me that a man-slave had stolen a canoe and escaped, taking Dian with him.

"He was a man from Suvi," said the chief. "I have forgotten his name."

"Was it Do-gad?" I asked.

"Yes," he said, "that was it. Do-gad was his name."

Once more my high hopes were dashed, and now my quest seemed hopeless and I was further harassed by the thought that Dian was again in the power of her nemesis. What was I to do? I had a sailboat, but I could not find the mainland, nor was there anyone to guide me to it.

Presently I conceived a forlorn hope, and going among the Ko-van slaves, I questioned each one, asking him from what country he came; and finally one of them, a girl, said she was from Suvi.

"Are there any other Suvian slaves here?" I asked.

"No," she said, "not since Do-gad escaped."

I went, then, to the chief of the Ruvans. "Ro-Tai," I said, "I have tried to serve you well. I have taught you how to catch the fish in the center of the pool. I have shown you how you may make your canoes go without paddling; and I have helped you to win two battles and take many slaves."

"Yes," he said, "you have done all these things, David. You are a good warrior."

"I want to ask a favor in return," I said.

"What is it?" he asked.

"I want you to promise to let me return to the mainland and my own country whenever I can."

He shook his head. "I cannot do that, David," he said. "You are now a Ruvan warrior, and no Ruvan may go to live in any other country."

"I have another favor to ask, then," I said, "that I think you will not find too difficult to grant."

"What is it?" he asked.

"I should like to have a slave," I said.

"Certainly," he agreed. "When we return to Ruva,

you may select one of the slaves that we have taken today."

"I do not want any that you have selected," I said. "I want that girl over there;" and I pointed to the slave from Suvi.

Ro-Tai raised his eyebrows and hesitated for a moment; but then he said, "Why not? You are both white. You should have a mate, and you cannot mate with a Ruvan."

Well, I would let him think what he pleased, just so long as I acquired a slave from Suvi.

I walked over to the girl. "You are my slave," I said. "Come with me. What is your name?"

"Lu-Bra," she said; "but I do not want to be your slave. I do not want to go with you. I belong to a woman here, and she is kind to me."

"I shall be kind to you," I said. "You need have no fear of me."

"But I still do not want to go with you. I would rather die."

"You are going with me, nevertheless, and you are not going to die, and you are not going to be harmed in any way. You may believe me that you are going to be very glad that I selected you."

Well, she had to come along with me. There was nothing she could do about it; but she was not very happy. I didn't want to tell her what I had in mind, for the success of the plan I had concocted depended solely upon the secrecy with which I could carry it out.

The warriors of Ruva ate in the village of the Ko-vans, who were their unwilling hosts; and then we returned to the ocean with our slaves and embarked for Ruva; and Lu-Bra, the slave-girl from Suvi, went with me.

The wind had risen since we landed on Ko-va; and now it was blowing half a gale and the seas were commencing to run high. It looked to me like a risky venture to embark in the face of such ominous weather; but the Ruvans seemed to think nothing of it. The wind had not only freshened but it had changed; so that now I could run directly before it, and our canoe fairly flew through the water. We didn't have to wait for the others this time, and they were soon specks far astern. The warriors who were fortunate enough to have been selected as the crew of this boat were highly enthusiastic. They had never travelled so fast before, and they had never travelled at all without hard work. Now they just sat idle and contented, and watched the waves go by.

But I was not so contented. My improvised mast and cordage were being subjected to terrific strain. There were creakings and squeakings that filled me with apprehension; and the sea and the wind were rising. I can tell you that I breathed a sigh of relief when I glimpsed Ruva in the distance, although there was still plenty of time for disaster to overtake us before we ran into one of her sheltering coves.

The sky was overcast with ominous clouds. The air about us was filled with spindrift. The wind howled and shrieked like malevolent demons seeking to terrify those whom they were about to destroy. The seas became mountainous. I glanced at my companions, and I was aware that for the first time they were showing marked concern. I was considerably worried myself, for I didn't see how this frail craft could possibly survive the fury of the storm. Why my sail and mast did not carry away, I still cannot conceive; but they held. The great following seas never quite engulfed us, and we drew rapidly nearer and nearer the shore.

As we came closer, I witnessed a strange and terrifying sight. The entire island, as far as I could see, was rising and falling as though in the throes of a terrific and continuous earthquake. Mountainous waves were breaking on the low shoreline and carrying tons of water into the forest. Pieces of the island were breaking off and disintegrating. How could we hope to make a landing under such conditions? And then Ro-Tai voiced that very doubt.

"We can't land here," he said. "We must try to make the lee side of the island."

I knew that that would be impossible. To change our course now would throw us into the trough of these enormous seas, and the craft would be capsized almost immediately. There was just one slender hope; and I held my course straight for that tossing, leaping shoreline.

We were almost upon it. I held my breath, and I imagine the Ruvans did likewise. We rose to the crest of a great sea. With my stone knife I cut the sheet, and the sail streamed out, flapping in the gale. We were only a few yards from the shore toward which we were rushing with the speed of an express train; and, for the few seconds that were required to assure the success of my mad scheme, the canoe clung to the crest of a great wave and we were carried inland and hurled among the trees of the forest.

Why no one was killed is still a mystery to me. Some were injured; but the rest of us managed to hold the canoe from being carried back into the ocean by the receding waters.

Before another large wave descended upon us, we stumbled deeper into the forest. We were being constantly hurled to the ground by the upheaval of the ground beneath us; and sometimes a wave would reach us but broken and rendered harmless by the trees of the forest.

At last we reached the village, where we found most of the huts lying collapsed upon the ground, while the Ruvans who had not accompanied the expedition, and the slaves, lay prone and terrified in the clearing.

My fear was that the entire island would disinte-

grate. I did not see how it could withstand the terrific forces that were wrenching at it, pulling it this
way and that, raising and lowering it, twisting and
turning it. I asked Ul-Van what he thought our
chances were.

"I have seen but one such storm before in my lifetime," he said. "Portions of the island were broken
off and lost; but the main part of the island withstood
the worst that wind and sea could do. If the storm
does not last too long, I think that we are safe."

"And what about the men in the other canoes?"
I asked.

Ul-Van shrugged. "Some of them may reach
shore," he said; "but it is more likely that none of
them ever will. It was your sail that saved us,
David."

⤜ 27 ⤛

THAT storm meant more to me than the destruction of Ruva or its menace to my own existence, for I knew that out there somewhere among those mountainous waves was Dian in a frail canoe. Her chances for survival seemed to me absolutely nonexistent. I tried to drive these destructive fears from my mind, and with the abating of the storm I partially succeeded; and hope was at last again renewed when the warriors we had given up for lost returned to the village. Not a canoe had been lost, nor not a man. It was a marvel of extraordinary seamanship.

The first concern of the Ruvans was to rebuild their

village; and in this work everyone joined, including the women and children. When this work was completed, I told Ro-Tai that I was going to repair the damage done to the sailing canoe. He asked me if I wanted any help, but I told him that I would need no one other than my slave, Lu-Bra. He did not insist upon my taking anyone else, nor did he put any watch over me this time. Evidently he had accepted me as a full-fledged member of the tribe; and so Lu-Bra and I went down to the seashore to commence our task.

Having found that I had no intention of harming her, the girl's spirits had returned and she seemed quite content and happy.

While I worked on the canoe, I had her gather food and prepare it. She also collected a supply of water from the trees, and filled bamboo containers with it. These things I hid in the forest near my work.

I made some bone fish-hooks for her, and taught her how to fish in the quiet waters of the inlet. The fish she caught, she smoked and dried and packed away for future use.

I did not acquaint her with my plan; but I had to

place some trust in her, as it was necessary to caution her to silence relative to our collection and storage of food and water. She asked no questions, and that was a good sign, for a person who asks no questions can usually keep his own counsel.

She had been a prisoner of the Ko-vans for a considerable period, probably for a number of years of outer earthly time. She had been there when Dian and Do-gad had been brought from the mainland, and had become well acquainted with Dian who told her that after she had escaped from the man-eating giants of Azar, she had also succeeded in escaping from Do-gad but that he had pursued her and that the very moment he had overtaken her they had both been captured by the Ko-vans.

I shuddered to think of all that my lovely Dian had been compelled to endure because her love for me had driven her forth in search of me. That she should die without knowing that I was comparatively safe seemed a cruel blow of Fate. She could not even know that I had escaped from the Jukans after I had left her in the cave and gone back to rescue Zor and Kleeto.

My work upon the canoe progressed nicely; but I was still highly impatient for the moment when I could put my plan into execution. The only danger now was that it might be discovered if some Ruvan stumbled upon our cache of food and water. I would have hard work explaining that away.

At last it was finished; and on the way back to the village I warned Lu-Bra to be sure not to mention this fact. "Certainly not," she said. "Do you think I want to give our plan away?"

Our plan! "Why do you call it our plan?" I asked. "You don't even know what I have in mind."

"Oh yes I do," she said; "and it is our plan, because I have worked and helped you."

"That is right," I said; "and whatever the plan is, it is ours together; and we will carry it out together, and we will say nothing about it to anyone else. Is that right?"

"Absolutely," she said.

"And what do you think the plan is?" I asked her.

"You are going back to the mainland in that canoe which goes without paddles; and you are taking me with you to point the direction to Suvi, because you cannot do it yourself. That is why you chose me from among the other slaves of Ko-va. I am not a fool, David. It is all quite plain to me, and you need have no fear that I shall divulge our secret to anyone."

I liked the use of the word "our." It almost assured her loyalty, even aside from anything else that she had said.

"I was very fortunate," I said.

"In what way?" she demanded.

"In finding you, instead of another slave, on Ko-va. You are intelligent and loyal, and you also know when you are well off. But how did you know that I could not find my way to the mainland without someone's help?"

"Who, in Suvi, does not know all about David, Emperor of Pellucidar?" she demanded. "Who does not know that he is from another world, and that he can do almost everything better than we of Pellucidar, but that if he is taken out of sight of familiar landmarks, he could never find his way home again? That is a marvel to us Pellucidarians, something which we cannot understand. It must be a strange world in which you lived, where no one dared go far from home, knowing that he could never find it again."

"But we do find our way around, even better than Pellucidarians," I said, "because we not only can find our way home, but we can find our way to any place in our world."

"That," she said, "is incomprehensible."

I had been working on the canoe very steadily, and, of course, there being no way of measuring time, I had no way of knowing how long we had been absent from the village. Having had our own food supply, we had eaten occasionally, but neither of us slept. The fact that both of us were very sleepy should have told us that we had been absent for a considerable period of time; and this must have been true, for when we returned we discovered that preparations had been almost completed for a huge feast to celebrate our victory over the Ko-vans. Everybody was very excited about it, but all that Lu-Bra and I wanted to do was to go to our huts and sleep.

O-Ra, who often sought my company when I was

in the village, asked me what in the world Lu-Bra and I could be doing to be away so much.

"We are working on the canoe that goes without paddles," I replied.

"I shall have to come with you the next time you go," she said, "because I have never seen it."

Well, that was just what I didn't want, because I had planned that the next time that Lu-Bra and I went to the canoe we would never return. We had only returned this time in order to get a good sleep before we set out upon our voyage; but I said, "That will be fine, O-Ra; but why don't you wait until I have finished it?"

"Oh, I can come then, too, and have a ride in it," she said. "Do you know, David, I wish that you were not white. I cannot imagine a finer mate than you. I think I shall ask Ro-Tai to make an exception in your case, so that I may be your mate."

"Because I have a slave?" I asked, laughing.

"No," she said. "I should get rid of Lu-Bra because I think you like her too well. I would not care to have a rival."

The young lady was quite frank. Sometimes these paleolithic maidens are; but not always. Dian had been just the opposite.

"Well," I said, "you may make somebody a fine mate, but not me. I already have one."

O-Ra shrugged. "Oh, you'll never see her again," she said. "You've got to live here all the rest of your life, and you might as well have a mate."

"Forget it, O-Ra," I said, "and pick out a nice man of your own race."

"Do you mean that you don't want me?" she demanded, angrily.

"It is not a question of wanting you or not wanting you," I replied. "It is that, as I told you before, I already have a mate; and in my country we never have but one at a time."

"That's not the reason," she snapped. "You're in love with Lu-Bra. That's why you go out together alone all the time. Any fool could see that."

"Well, have it your own way, O-Ra," I said. "I'm going to get some sleep now;" and I turned and left her.

When I awoke I was thoroughly rested; and,

shortly after, Lu-Bra awoke. When we came out of the hut we saw that they were already gathering for the feast. I was ravenously hungry and wanted to eat, and I knew that Lu-Bra must want to also. The fact that a feast was going on gave us an excellent opportunity to escape without detection, since every member of the tribe would be in the village during the feast, and there would be no likelihood of anyone discovering us while we launched the canoe and loaded it up with our supplies.

I suggested this to Lu-Bra. "I think we can get out of here, now, without being seen," I said. "They will think that we are still asleep in our hut, if they miss us, which they may not."

"Good," she said. "We can keep the huts between us and them until we enter the forest;" and so we bade farewell to the village of the Ru-vans for what we hoped would be the last time.

We hurried to the canoe; and, with our combined efforts, managed finally to drag it into the water; then we hastened to load it with our provisions.

We had just about completed our work when I saw someone approaching through the forest from the di-

rection of the village. It was too late now to conceal
what we were doing, and I knew that whoever it was
would know what we were contemplating the moment that they saw us loading the canoe with water
and food.

Lu-Bra was returning from the cache with her arms
full, and I was just starting back for another load,
when O-Ra burst upon the scene.

"So that's what you're doing," she flared, angrily.
"You are going to run away, and you are going to
take that white-faced thing with you."

"You guessed it the first time, O-Ra," I said.

"Well, you're not going to do it. I'll see to that,"
she snapped. "But if you want to escape from Ruva,
I'll go with you instead of that girl. If you won't do
that, I'll give the alarm."

"But I have to take Lu-Bra," I said. "Otherwise,
I could never find the mainland." I thought maybe
by explaining I could mollify her. "You know, O-Ra,
that you could not show me how to reach the mainland."

"Very well, take her along, too, then, as guide; but
I am going as your mate."

"No, O-Ra," I said. "I am sorry; but that would not work out."

"You won't take me?" she asked.

"No, O-Ra."

Her eyes flashed angrily for a moment, and then she turned and walked back into the forest. It seemed to me that she had given up very easily.

Lu-Bra and I hurried as fast as we could to load the remainder of our provisions in the canoe. We couldn't afford to leave without taking everything that we had collected, for we had no idea how long we would be on the water before we reached the mainland.

We had stowed away the last load, and Lu-Bra had taken her place in the canoe, when I heard the sounds of approaching men; and I knew that O-Ra had returned to the village and reported what she had discovered. I pushed off and paddled away from shore just as forty or fifty Ruvan warriors burst into sight. Ro-Tai was in the lead, and he shouted to me to come back; but I turned the nose of the canoe toward the open sea and started to hoist the sail. There was a slight off-shore wind, and it seemed an eternity before the sail caught the little breeze that reached us. Both Lu-Bra and I paddled frantically; but if we did not get more wind we never could escape the Ruvans, who were now piling into their canoes to take up the pursuit.

The leading canoe shot out from the shore; but now we were far enough out so that we were catching a little more wind and moving just a little more rapidly. However, they were overhauling us; and all the time Ro-Tai was shouting for me to come back; and his canoe was drawing nearer.

They came within a spear-throw of us; but now we were holding about even. Ro-Tai stood up in the canoe with his spear poised to throw.

"Come back," he said, "or you die!"

Lu-Bra had crossed from Ko-va in the canoe, and since then she had asked many questions relative to its handling. Whether or not she could steer it I didn't know, but I had to take the chance; and so I called her to me and told her to take the steering paddle; then I fitted an arrow to my bow and stood up.

"Ro-Tai, I do not want to kill you," I said; "but if you don't lay down that spear I shall have to."

He hesitated a moment. A gust of wind bellied our sail bravely, and the canoe leaped ahead just as Ro-Tai hurled his weapon. I knew that it would fall short; and so I did not shoot him, for I liked Ro-Tai and he had been kind to me.

"Do not forget, Ro-Tai," I called back, "that I could have killed you but that I did not. I am your friend; but I want to return to my own country."

We were pulling away from them rapidly now. For awhile they followed us; but, seeing the futility of further pursuit, they at last turned back.

≍ 28 ≍

HOW long that voyage lasted, God only knows. A dozen times we were attacked by huge nameless monsters, and three times we ran into storms that threatened to terminate our voyage and our lives simultaneously; but somehow we pulled through, until at last we were faced with the knowledge that our food and water would soon be gone.

Lu-Bra proved to be a very wonderful girl. She was courageous and uncomplaining. I felt sorry for her.

"You would have been better off on Ruva, Lu-Bra," I said. "It is commencing to look very much as though I had led you to death instead of to freedom."

"Whatever happens, I am content, David," she said. "I would rather be dead than a slave."

"Your being with me is a strange coincidence, Lu-Bra, which I have never before mentioned. It was another girl from Suvi who was going to lead me toward Sari. We were both prisoners of the Jukans, and then of the man-eating giants of Azar. Whether she died there or escaped them, I do not know."

"What was her name?" asked Lu-Bra.

"Kleeto," I said.

"I knew her," said Lu-Bra. "We were children together, before I was stolen."

On and on we sailed, Lu-Bra, my living compass, pointing the way. We had rationed the food to a point where we had barely enough to sustain life, and only two or three sips of water a day. We were both weak and emaciated. We had had poor luck with our fishing, possibly because neither one of us was from a maritime nation. On land, I could have brought in plenty of game; but out here on the water, although it teemed with food, I seemed scarcely ever to make a direct hit. Why that should have been,

I do not know, for I have become an excellent shot with bow-and-arrow.

After the last morsel of food was consumed we made a catch with one of my bone fishhooks. It was a little fish about a foot long; but we cut it in two and devoured it raw. Shortly after this, our water supply was exhausted. I prayed for another storm with rain; but the sky remained clear, and the merciless noonday sun beat down upon us; and across that wide expanse of unfriendly ocean there was no sign of land.

Lu-Bra was lying under her shelter in the bottom of the canoe. She spoke to me in a weak voice. "David," she asked, "are you afraid to die?"

"I do not want to die," I replied; "but I am not afraid to. Possibly it is another wonderful adventure in which we shall go to a new country and meet new people and many of our old friends who have gone before us, and after awhile we shall all be gathered there."

"I hope so, David," she said, "for I am dying now. I hate to desert you, David, for companionship is all either of us have left now. When I am gone, you will be alone; and it is not good to die alone."

I turned away my head to hide the tears that came to my eyes, and as I did so I saw something that brought an exclamation of astonishment and incredulity to my lips. It was a sail!

What was a sail doing upon that ocean where there could be no sails? And then a possibility of the truth dawned upon me.

"Lu-Bra!" I cried. "You shall not die. We are saved, Lu-Bra."

"What do you mean, David?" she asked. "Land?"

"No," I said, "a sail; and if this is the Lural Az, as you have told me it must be, it can only be a friendly sail."

I changed our course and headed for the strange ship, which I soon saw was bearing down upon us. They must have seen our sail, too. As we came nearer I recognized the vessel as one of the type that Perry had designed and built after his first disastrous attempt to build a battleship. I could have wept for joy.

I lowered our sail and waited. The little vessel hove to beside us and tossed me a line, and as I looked up into the faces peering down from above,

I recognized Ja the Mezop who had commanded one of the first vessels of our fleet.

"David!" he cried. "You? It has been hundreds of sleeps since we gave you up for dead."

Lu-Bra was too weak to clamber aboard Ja's vessel. She could only raise herself to a sitting position, and I was too weak to help her; but willing hands soon lifted us both aboard; and as I reached the deck a woman ran toward me and threw her arms about me. It was Dian the Beautiful.

After they had given us a little food and water and we were somewhat revived and strengthened, Dian told me her story.

She had helped Do-gad escape from Ko-va, on Do-gad's explicit promise that he would respect her and help her to return to Sari; but he had broken his word to her, and she had killed him. Of this metal are the beautiful daughters of Amoz.

Then she had paddled on toward the mainland, guided unerringly by her homing instinct. She had evidently been out of the track of the great storm which I had feared must have spelled her doom; but she had passed safely through the three storms that Lu-Bra and I had encountered.

We are back in Sari now, contented and happy. Lu-Bra was returned to Suvi; and the warriors who escorted her brought back word that made me still happier, and also gave me some slight idea as to the length of time that I was a prisoner on Ruva, for the word that they brought me was that Zor and Kleeto had reached Suvi safely, and that they had mated and already had a little son.

THE END

In the Bison Frontiers of Imagination series

University of Nebraska Press